I, The Mummy © Roy Lester Pond 2018.

Book 1

Egypt's mythic avenger

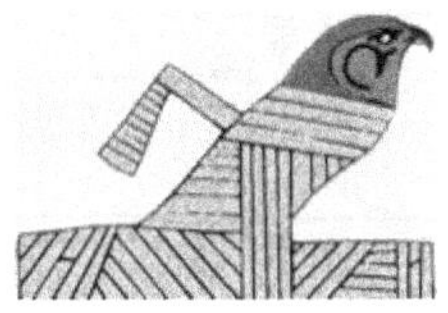

CHAPTER 1

At the corners of my eyes I saw loose threads of cloth frayed with age turn into blazing filaments of light.

Sunlight!

I was lying in the darkness of a sepulchre, yet rays of light had found me.

The priests had come and they had awakened the monkey first.

I felt the tiny weight of the creature squatting on my chest as rays of heat struck the bindings around my stretched out body.

I drew a breath of air into my dried up lungs like a hiss of sand in a windstorm, forced my eyelids open, cracking a seal of dust and time. Light roared in my skull. My eyes cowered at the shining fire as I peered out through gaps in frayed linen bandaging.

The daylight sun of Ra and of Egypt, the Land of the Living, enveloped me in an embrace of life, while the fragrance of death's embalming ointments and oils lingered in my nostrils.

I saw a solar priest standing apart, holding up an angled copper mirror, catching a beam of sunlight flashed to him from another priest standing further back along a passage with another mirror beyond him, and then another - a relay of priests with mirrors stepping back to infinity it seemed, flashing light rays between them from the world of the living above, funneling it down the lengths of passages to the place where I lay in the earth.

The little monkey mummy, Thoth, had its back to me, holding up its paws to greet the shooting beams of sunlight as if in reverence, or warming itself in a new dawning.

Was this a tomb?

An open, hawk-headed coffin stood near me and I found that I was lying on my back on a stone slab.

I saw other things.

An old man with gold dust on his skin like the flesh of Ra, standing over my body. A higher priest this one, shining like Ra at his noonday height, wearing a golden collar of a High Priest of Ra.

This may be a tomb, but I was not being buried, I sensed.

It was more than a tomb.

Swords, battle-axes, clubs, shields, bows and arrows crammed alcoves in the walls...

A sanctuary filled with weapons of war.

The sunlight assaulting my eyes ripped apart the cobwebs of forgetfulness and revealed a blinding truth, a *recollection that was like another blazing sun hitting me.*

I was a warrior who had fought in a battle against demonic demigod attackers and I had fallen on the battlefield.

And along with this knowledge came another memory, reminding me of a dark absence, opening up a void as large as this chamber... the consciousness of a parting from a loved one left behind... long ago... how long ago? *I had died not only to a great land racked by turmoil, but also to a great love.*

Her name was Mehyt...

"Arise, Great Hori, arise from the hold of death," the High Priest said in a voice that echoed in the sepulchre. "Arise, Defender of Egypt, warrior hero of the primordial wars of men against the rule of the demon demigods. Arise, Hori, the semi-divine, last of the line of mighty Horus the warrior god who avenged the murder of his father Osiris. You are called upon in this hour of Egypt's peril to save a land that has dire need of your might."

The monkey on my chest chattered in excitement.

I tried to speak, but my jaws were grinding stones and a single word escaped my throat.

"Then…"

"You died and were entombed in this sanctuary over a thousand years ago."

Thousand?

That made me an orphan to a long dead past, a reborn seedling sprouted from ancient grain to a new life in an alien soil.

With a straining effort of will, I ground out more words. "Then am I a Helpless One?"

A mummy, a dried up husk? An empty chrysalis after life had escaped like a moth.

"Far from helpless. You are a being magically transformed, raised from death into new power," the ministering priest said, "for like the god Osiris, your body was wrapped in the *Tresses of Nephthys,* the magical bandages of linen woven on a sacred loom by the goddess Nephthys, sister of Isis. And over those wrappings, you wear a magical outer band woven by the Queen of Heaven herself. The magical *Knotted Cords of Isis…* the cord that links life to death. An ancestor of demigods, you are a buried weapon hidden until Egypt had need to raise you again like a sheathed sword as the oracles foretold. And now is such a time of need. I, Ra-Hotep, First Prophet of Holy Ra raise you in Ra's light to wage a great and holy battle against a new enemy."

"Enemy?"

"A vile foreign power, the Hyksos, Asiatic Rulers of Foreign Lands, have occupied Egypt with plans of an empire. They seek to plunder Egypt's forbidden treasure of secrets for themselves - and you alone can stop them."

"Holy Egypt conquered." I groaned. "How?"

My love of the Red and Black Land had not died. It burnt like a flame inside me.

"Your eyes shall see, Hori," the Chief Prophet Of Ra said. "But first gather your strength. Allow Ra's beneficent rays of fire to revivify your limbs. Then you may rise to this new age of war, though taking care never to shed your armour of divine bands. The *Tresses of Nephthys* and the *Knotted Cords of Isis* around your body are the secrets of your strength and miraculous preservation."

The world turned as I brought thousands of years of horizontality to the vertical and stood up, placing my feet back on mother Egypt again, even though in a cavern below her surface.

Shakily, with the monkey clinging to my shoulder, supportive priests at either side of me walked me haltingly along the lengths of passages and hallways of my tomb sanctuary and up steps to a blazing rectangle of light, a doorway to the world.

What waited for me outside was a sight as amazing as the day.

Two stamping black steeds stood tethered to an enclosed platform on wheels.

A war chariot, I learnt, and my first sight of such an astonishing machine.

"Stolen from the enemy, a weapon of their construction that they used to devastating effect to bring sweeping ruin to the armies of Egypt."

They lifted me into the chariot where I clung to a rail beside a dark-skinned driver. The young man of Nubian descent, his skull shaven like a priest's, gaped at me. My face, visible between bonds had only begun to reclaim the semblance and colour of life.

We set off, the breeze fluttering the wrappings around my face.

The High Priest followed in a carrying chair born by his priests.

We crossed a plain of blinding fallen sunlight and climbed to heights.

We stopped and my driver helped me to the ground.

"We must not be seen from the plain below, Great Hori," my driver said as we waited for the priest to join us "I am Harka, a temple keeper of the god and a soldier priest, but one with only a shadow of your skills as a warrior."

"What are we here to see?" My voice grated like a whisper of doom.

"The scene of a battle against Egypt's vile occupiers."

"Who are these Hyksos?"

"Bearded warriors from regions of the east who swept in with chariots and armies from the desert to seize the Delta and overpower us, burn our cities, raze temples of the gods to the ground, and treat the people with cruel hostility, massacring many, and leading into slavery the wives and children of others... They made a vassal of our king in Thebes, forcing him to pay tribute and taxes. Their capital is a new city of Avaris in the Delta, but the usurper is pushing south. Now pharaoh Seqenenre Tao has brought an army from Thebes to meet him and you will witness his fortune in a battle from these heights."

I detected a note of gloom.

"You do not sound hopeful."

"The oracles are dark. Like the Hyksos king whose name is Apophis."

Apophis? Apophis was the name of the evil underworld serpent of outer darkness that threatened to swallow the sun god Ra each night and as he traveled through darkness.

"What ruler would bear such a name?"

"One who is as twisted as the great serpent himself. This battle you will witness today is the result of a new and insulting demand from this twisted king. He provoked hostilities by sending an emissary from his capital in the Delta all the way to the Egyptian king in far-off Thebes with this message: "Remove the hippopotamuses from your canal in the east of the city. The noise they make by day and night is in my ears and is keeping me from my sleep."

A preposterous demand, I thought, designed in its twisted indirection to stupefy the Egyptians. A joke? A threat? A subtle declaration of war?

"Asiatic sand-dwellers!" The young priestly guard spat on the ground. "A foreign stain on holy Egypt... and this king has dark ambitions beyond worldly power, but it is not for me to speak of that. Ra-Hotep, the High Priest will tell you."

"Keep low, they must not see us."

Under the High Priest's instruction, I crawled in the sand to the edge of the heights and even the golden High Priest lowered himself under Ra's brilliant light and crept up beside me on his belly.

Below us on the plain, the rising dust-clouds of two armies drew towards each together, brewing like opposing sandstorms.

From the south, the forces of Upper Egypt and the tall king Seqenenre Tao, visible among his royal bodyguard in his blue crown and armour of hard gems, flanked by spearmen, axe men and clubmen and wings of Nubian mercenary bowmen.

From the north, an army such as I had never seen. Men in a horde of horse drawn chariots, soldiers protected in mailed shirts of metal and metal helmets and alien, curved swords like sickles.

Around them washed a sea of archers with curved and thickened bows.

The Hyksos army was out of range of the Egyptian archers, but astonishingly commenced hostilities by releasing a hail of arrows from a vast distance that sped across the gap between them and swarmed on the Egyptian forces like attacking wasps.

The Egyptian army roared in alarm.

Men dropped like insects all around.

"They bring bows hardened with layers of wood, horn and sinew and their arrows can span twice the distance of ours. And they have weapons of hardened bronze. Sickle swords that shatter our copper blades."

Now the chariot horde broke from the line and ran in a spear shaped advance, the infantry surging behind them.

They gathered speed, hurtling missiles of man, metal and animal, stocked with infantry and archers shooting as they came, the sun spangling on brazen sickle swords, spears and battle-axes.

The Egyptians broke their line and fanned out in an attempt to enclose the chariots in a bull-horn trap, but withering Hyksos fire decimated their numbers on each side.

The foreigners hit.

The priestly observers beside me on the heights gasped. The attackers had swept away the Egyptian king's royal bodyguard, leaving Seqenenre Tao exposed, and allowing an axe man in a chariot to strike a blow at the forehead of the blue-crowned pharaoh.

Seqenenre Tao threw out his arms as though in a gesture of defeat and hit the sand.

Following chariots disgorged soldiers, one with a mace and they struck at the king's head again and again in hateful overkill.

The sandstorm from the north swallowed the dust storm from the south and the sight of it left me trembling with anger.

"Oh, if only you had been down there in your full strength, Great Hori," the young warrior priest Harka said. "You would have crushed the Hyksos army into the sand."

It was the kind of boastful propaganda that warrior rulers liked portraying on temple wall carvings, showing themselves in giant size reliefs smiting a helpless enemy that tumbled in disarray at their feet.

Was it mockery, or did the young man have a touching and boundless belief in me?

The monkey at my head gibbered softly.

To the others, it was just a monkey chattering, but the creature was a familiar of Thoth, the shrewd god of wisdom and of words, and a small voice of conscience that goaded me.

"One man against an army, My Master? Do not let flattery deceive. Once a hero, you are no better than a Helpless One who must crawl on the sand. A man in tatters. You must gather your strength to be a hero again."

"Your eyes have seen enough," the High Priest said. "Now I will tell you what you must do to save our land. Come with me and we shall speak."

We crawled back from the edge until it was safe to rise again.

He took me apart and we sat on a rocky outcrop on the heights away from all other ears except those of the monkey, who squatted on my shoulder eavesdropping on the priest's words, its eyes in close-set attention.

How was I, one risen warrior, versed in the ways of wars that were a thousand years old, going to save this land? The demigods had been mighty enemies, but the Hyksos army was a war machine, armed with bewildering new weapons and they fought in a manner that was as foreign to me as they were.

I felt my age that day.

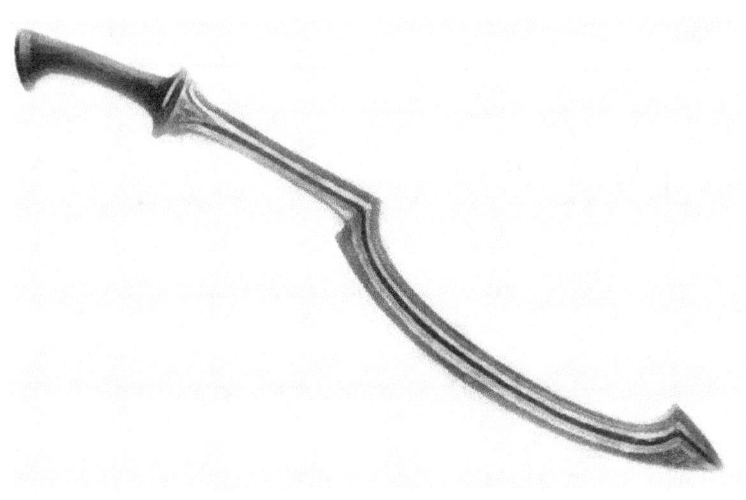

Khopesh sword

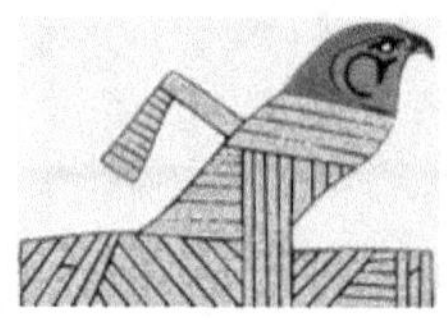

CHAPTER 2

"The world has changed," I said. "It is a new world of fearsome arms."

"And fearsome evil. The Hyksos King Apophis, one in a line of Hyksos usurpers, worships but one god and one god only, renouncing all others. Never has it been so before. The Hyksos ruler worships the darkest god of all, Seth, warlike god of deserts and raging storms, murderer of the good god Osiris who hacked the body of his brother Osiris into pieces. King Apophis has built a great temple to Seth in his capital of Avaris to sacrifice to the dark god each day. This is more than an invasion of empires."

"What is it?"

"The re-enactment on earth of a cosmic drama. As above, so below. Apophis, like the underworld serpent of darkness, has swallowed Ra, the sun of Egypt. Egypt lies in darkness, fragmented, cut into pieces like the body of Osiris. But the conqueror's soothsayers warn

Apophis that Egypt dreams of resurrection. There is only one sure way to stop us. He must find and seize the tools of resurrection, the great hidden Secret of Osiris, the secret of how Isis resurrected Osiris – before we do. It is a secret of resurrection that he wants for himself. The Asiatic king hungers for the forbidden knowledge of Egypt and his scribes have been commissioned to raid and copy Egyptian texts for himself."

"Then what must I do?"

"Stop Apophis. Stop him from finding the potent tools of power that he seeks. Find them first - or seize them from them by force of arms."

"What then?"

"Ra's servants will turn them against him. We shall use these tools of great power to resurrect Egypt in a magical ceremony of re-enactment that will echo the drama of Osiris, the process of gathering, unification and binding together of the severed land and so magically begin the resurrection Egypt, just as the goddesses Isis and Nepthys bound together the parts of the body of Osiris in wrappings and raised him from the dead using the magic of their incantations."

"What are these tools of power?"

"You must secure three caches of relics, all keys to the Osiris resurrection. Two of these relics of power lie buried in the Delta, hidden inside the lost tombs of Nephthys and Isis. One cache contains the last remaining *Tresses of Nephthys* and the other the magical *Knotted Cords of Isis* along with her funerary amulets. These tombs lie in the Delta stronghold of the Hyksos. The third relic is hidden in the Nome of the god Thoth, at the base of the flower of the Delta, where the Hyksos are now spreading their rule. Inside a sanctuary of Thoth lies a scroll of spells used by Isis to revive Osiris. You must find and secure all three holy treasures to save Egypt."

"How much time do I have?"

"Precious little. Apophis is searching for the relics, sending out armed missions from his garrisons, scouring the land that, as each day goes by, he gains more control of, guided by a Hyksos priest of Seth named Sutekhy. You will need all the power you can bring from the beyond to defeat him. Sutekhy is a magician and a seer, a scryer of flames, and he will be using his magic to try to see your every move and to know the secrets of your heart." He paused and rested a sympathetic hand on my shoulder. "And there is another reason why you must hasten."

"What reason? "

"When Isis and Nephthys raised Osiris it was only for a brief time before he ascended to his kingship of the afterlife. So it is with you. You have risen for a time, Hori, but your life cannot be prolonged indefinitely and you must return to your rest in the tomb."

"Then my immortality is a curse."

The priest nodded.

"Yet a blessing for Egypt. When you have gathered all of the relics, have Harka send a message to me and I will meet you later in Abydos for the apotheosis that will mark the ending of Egypt's affliction... "

We returned to the sanctuary.

"Harka will be your right arm," the High Priest said. "Along with the chariot and horses which you can stable in the cavern beside your sanctuary, he has a cache of Hyksos weapons for you to use as you regain your powers. He has my priestly authority to provide for all your needs and knows how to send word to me through others. Save us, Hori. Holy Egypt depends on your might for you have great new powers beyond mortal men that you bring from the world beyond."

Powers from beyond...

Yes, I had those.

New powers, just as the stolen Hyksos weapons were new to my experience of war.

As my strength built under the sun, the priest soldier put me through my paces.

He handed me an Egyptian shield and a copper straight sword and he took a Hyksos bronze scimitar and bronze studded shield for himself.

"The *khopesh* sword, hardened bronze made by adding tin to copper," he said. "Crooked and devious, like king Apophis. Come at me."

The Egyptian straight sword in my hand brought back a weight of memories, a thousand clashes with demon demigods who fought to rule over humankind at the end of the age of the gods, shape-shifters who could escape an attack by cascading into the forms of animals, beings in a state of constant flux, one moment a human-headed foe, another moment a head of a ram with spiral-galaxy horns, or a jackal or an angry falcon...

Forget them now.

Harka, my sparring partner, was circling, protected behind his bronze shield, moving so that he could strike behind my round-topped shield of cowhide and wood.

Or so I thought. He leapt to bypass my shield. I raised my shield as his blow came, but he aimed not for my body.

He hooked the top of my shield with the blunt section of his sword in the dent before the curve of the blade and gave a mighty haul that almost ripped it out of my hand.

The sickle sword was also a hook.

He ripped the shield down, exposing my head and chest and he swung his sword around in an arc to come down on my copper blade, smashing it in half and leaving me exposed and powerless.

He threw me a grin.

"You try."

The sun was burning me now, searing into my joints, loosening stiffness, feeding the energy of Ra into long dormant muscles.

He gave me his Hyksos sword and shield and took more Hyksos weapons for himself.

I hefted the new sword. A slashing weapon, but a good weight. Crooked in my hand, like the serpent Apophis. A cruel curve for a blade.

We sparred, made feints, looked for openings.

He swung. I blocked.

Our blades clashed with a mighty clangour without breaking, even though the force jarred our arms.

He lunged again at my shield.

But I was quicker.

My *khopesh* flashed down, hooked the top of his shield.

I hauled.

Harka was gripping his shield handle tightly, perhaps too tightly. The power of my tug snapped him forward and to the ground, the force so great that I could barely jump out of his way as he went rolling head over heels like a spinning ball before ending up smashing into rocks ten body lengths away.

The little monkey jumped up and down, chattering gleefully.

Harka got up, groggy, parting with a confused grin.

"Your powers are back…"

They were growing under the sun.

I tried Hyksos archery next.

Harka gave me a compound bow, showed me the glued layers of wood horn and sinew that gave the belly of the weapon its strength.

"To achieve its power and kill-distance the Hyksos take a year to make each one," he said. "It can shoot arrows with larger heads of bronze and greater power to penetrate enemy defences."

He gave me a quiver of bronze-tipped Hyksos arrows and set up a bronze-lined Hyksos shield as a target in the distance. For his part, he took an Egyptian bow and arrows from my sanctuary.

He went first, his first two arrows falling hopelessly short of the target. He bent the bow further and landed an arrow creditably close to its centre with a distant *thwack.*

Now I took aim, drew the arrow to the anchor point at my chin and released.

It blurred across the sand and while we heard a bang, we lost sight of the arrow.

Had it glanced off the surface?

I shot another with the same effect.

We paced towards the target together.

Harka's arrow came into view, sticking out of the shield. At closer inspection it had penetrated half way down its copper head.

Harka smiled and lifted the shield.

My two arrows had penetrated the shield, punching through the bronze and burying their shafts in the sand behind.

The narrow bladed Hyksos battle axe, of the kind that had felled Seqenenre Tao in the battle, was another revelation to me.

"The socket penetrating axe," Harka said. "See, the blade and the socket are made in one solid piece for a penetrating blow no Egyptian axe can match."

I gave it a swing.

A devastating weapon.

In my risen state in a new world, I had been given new powers and new weapons, and these were not my only advantages as I came to see.

I discovered other powers that had come with me from my realm of beyond.

I could hear the whispers of the dead coming from unknown tombs that lay hidden nearby.

And when I walked back in to the tomb sanctuary, I discovered that I had the ability to see without light in the darkness.

Harka used a flint to light a torch, but I had no need of its flame.

I could see into the darkest corners of the sanctuary.

"You are a being magically transformed, raised from death into new power," the ministering priest had said.

CHAPTER 3

At dusk we set off in the chariot for the Hyksos occupied region of the Delta.

I would begin by hunting for the tombs and relics of the goddesses Nephthys and Isis, leaving the Scroll in the Nome of Thoth for our return journey.

The priests had provided well for us, giving me a Hyksos hooded robe to conceal my wrappings and a woven coat and cowl for the monkey.

I took the reins for a time, not only because I needed to gain skills with the fast moving war machine, but because my eyes could see the desert terrain as clearly as if lit by a pale green flame, even on this moonless night.

"The Hyksos forces are everywhere," Harka said, "more so after the massing of the southerners under the fateful uprising of Seqenenre Tao. The Hyksos have even washed like an evil wave over the Nome of Thoth."

The monkey on my shoulder enjoyed the ride.

"Faster, My Master. We race the sun as it travels through the underworld to dawn to reach the Delta before daybreak."

I had fought many a battle in the Delta region in an age long gone and I knew it well, but not the site of the relics.

My priestly warrior companion was curious.

"What do we seek?"

He was part priest and invested with the High Priest's authority and must surely guess the answer. Perhaps he was testing me.

Whether the High Priest approved or not, there was no point in keeping my 'right hand' in darkness and it was a chance to share confidences and build our bond. In spite of his faith in my might, I needed an ally since I did not underestimate the danger of the zone we were entering or the lethal power of the enemy.

"First I must find a relic in the tomb of Nephthys, before Apophis does," I said.

"Nephthys, sister of Isis. What relic?"

"A coffer of wrappings."

"More wrappings, Great Hori." He looked up into my face in the cowl. "Surely you and the monkey have enough between you?"

The Nubian possessed a wit, I was learning.

"A golden coffer filled with a batch of the same consecrated wrappings that Nephthys wove for the resurrection of Osiris. Holy wrappings of great power."

"Tools for a resurrection? Whose?"

"That is a mystery I may not speak about."

Whose resurrection?

Not the king Apophis upon his eventual death, as he might be planning.

Not Osiris the god, as he had already been raised to become Ruler of the underworld.

No, it was for the resurrection of a land, a beloved, divided land.

Then the idea came.

It sniffed at the edges of my thoughts like a jackal of the dead on the edges of a necropolis.

These tools could resurrect another...

One lost to me... who lived and died in an age long past.

Mehyt, Chief Chantress in the temple of Ra.

The beloved of my heart. My lioness.

She had gone to her rest, her death unknown and unmourned by me as I slept in my sanctuary of weapons.

I remembered a night of passionate and sweet union between us when we swore that we would be together for eternity.

The monkey grumbled.

"What is it you dream of, My Master? Raise the dead in fond memory, yes, but in reality, no! You have a land to save. Not a love."

I had barely thought it, but the ape guessed.

The wise, chattering monkey that took its name from the god of knowledge.

Did I dare dream of saving Mehyt?

No.

It was a distraction and a distortion of my great commission.

Remember Egypt and the Hyksos battle axe falling on the skull of the Egyptian king, I told myself.

And yet...

Mehyt, sweet perfumed Mehyt... her lingering kisses on my mouth. Her whispering breath in my ear, the drowning slashes of her dark eyes, her golden arms that seemed to squeeze the breath from me.

Somewhere in the darkness of the Delta, her body lay asleep in its House of Eternity, waiting...

Would I hear her whisper calling to me?

My heart leapt.

We rode on through the night.

They broke from the cover of a ridge masked by the dazzle of a splintering dawn.

Two chariots with drivers and a soldier in each.

I handed the reigns to Harka and took the Hyksos bow from my shoulder.

"Keep low," I told him.

An arrow buzzed between us, a sound like ripping wind.

Monkey shrieked and took shelter on the floor of the chariot.

The attackers split in a fork to spread the target they presented to us, yet remained behind the sun's glare.

They thought the sun would blind me.

But my eyes that could see in darkness could also see through the fire of the sun.

I nocked a bronze tipped arrow to the bow.

I drew back, bending the powerful belly of wood, horn and sinew, aimed for the helmeted archer who was about to bend his bow, then switched aim to his driver.

I released. My arrow struck him in the shoulder of his mailed shirt, sent him lurching against the archer, spoiling his aim.

A returning arrow slammed into the wooden rail of our chariot.

The wounded Hyksos driver's tug on the reins caused the horses to veer towards the other chariot, which took evasive action, a swerve spoiling their aim.

"Pass between them and turn back!" I said to Harka.

The wounded driver, clinging to the reins took the horses in a tight turn.

Calamitously tight.

I heard a Hyksos curse.

A wheel hit a ridge, lifted the chariot, flung it to the sky, wheels spinning.

The chariot crashed on its side, the panicked horses hauling it around in a great slewing circle of spraying sand.

We flicked between our attackers and rounded. I went for the next chariot, penetrating the bronzed shirt of the warrior with an arrow. He spun out of the chariot and hit the sand.

I removed his driver with my next arrow.

We closed with the fallen chariot.

The first driver lay inert in the sand, but his armed warrior had managed to jump clear.

He roared at us, shaking his bronzed shield and battle axe.

"Stop," I told Harka.

I leapt down, armed with a Hyksos sword.

The sight of it surprised the black bearded Asiatic who stood near the fallen chariot, but it did not dismay him.

"Prepare to return to the hell you came from," he said in a snarl.

He knew.

How?

Had the magician priest of Seth, the scryer of flames, Sutecky, divined my awakening, overlooking my movements in his flames of divination?

While I drew upon the power beyond, the Hyksos used dark forces of magic.

We circled.

This duel would not be the same as sparring with the priest-soldier Harka.

Here was a warrior trained in Hyksos arms, likely the victor of a hundred combats.

What did he think of his hooded adversary now that he was close enough to look into my face, see my eyes between the wrappings of Nephthys?

He made a jab with his sword. I shifted aside to avoid his attack. It was a feint.

I needed to unnerve him.

"I have survived hell," I said. "You will not."

I saw a shadow pass across the black-pebble eyes.

"Wretch in wrappings. We'll see how you fare when I take your cloth head from your shoulders."

He was too wary to let me hook away his shield with my sword.

Sickle sword meets penetrating axe.

I glimpsed Thoth dancing on our chariot rail, the figure of Harka watching, stiffly immobile.

I watched for any movement from the hulking figure in front of me.

I noticed the upper wheel of the upset chariot still turning slowly after the crash.

He took a step, another feint. I raised my blade.

But he wasn't planning to strike at me. He struck at my sword instead, swinging hard.

The *khopesh* was made from hardened bronze, but it was no match for the dense, penetrative power of the Hyksos axe.

My sword shattered, leaving me with nothing but a blunt handle.

"Ha. Now you have only your wrappings to hide behind, Egyptian."

I was defenceless.

He had turned the battle.

Turned.

The slowly turning wheel.

He came to finish me off.

I dived. Not at him, but onto the wheel, grabbing it with stiffened arms and rotated myself in a blurring circle that brought me behind him.

I kicked out.

The force threw him reeling to the ground. I dived in his back. He spun, but I had taken the Hyksos dagger from my belt and used the narrow, mid-ribbed blade to strike between the bronze scales of armour.

"Go into the shadows, Hyksos!" I said in a grated whisper.

Monkey shrieked.

Harka gave a grunt of justification as much as satisfaction.

"I expected no less from the Great Hori."

We collected the enemy weapons and arrows to add them to our armoury and continued north.

I gaped at a sight across the Nile.

A cluster of mountains, smooth with triangular flat sides and shining, pointed tips, erupted from the plateau across the river, mountains that had never met my eyes before, touching the heavens.

"Has Egypt grown mountains while I slept?" I said.

"They are pyramids, tombs built by our kings a thousand years ago."

A thousand years, again.

The age of the wrappings around my body, rusted and dry, told the story.

I was a warrior from a primordial age, a doom-wrapped scroll unleashed on Egypt's oppressors like an ancient curse.

Nephthys mourning

CHAPTER 4

We passed by *On*, at the base of the lotus flower of the Nile Delta and entered a valley.

"How is it that you know where to look for the secret resting place of Nephthys?" Harka said.

"I don't. But I hear her whisperings from her tomb."

It was like the fluttering of a breeze in my ears.

Her whisperings spoke about the tresses that surrounded my body, the wrappings of woven linen that held me.

"I go round about you to protect you, Warrior Hori. I have come to be a protector to you. My strength shall be near you, my strength shall be near you, for ever..."

We were nearing the resting place of Nephthys, for though a goddess, after ruling Egypt for thousands of years, the gods had left their bodies to exist in the spiritual world. All things had an end, every god, every goddess, every man, every woman, every creature... all things except the High God.

And I, the mummy.

How had I survived death?

Or was it death?

Perhaps I had not truly died in the fullest sense, but lain in stasis wrapped in the preserving *Tresses of Nephthys* and the magical *Knotted Cords of Isis*, ready to be awakened when Egypt's time of need came.

"We are close," I said.

I heard the cry of a kite, her symbol, the ghostly mournful shriek of the Egyptian hawk.

The shriek grew louder, clearer.

"Nephthy is here," I said.

We came to a place where great rocks had tumbled from a hillside.

Harka stopped and we jumped to the ground.

"Nephthys is under here?"

"Yes. I am certain."

"We'd need an army of workmen to move it."

"Stand clear."

I grabbed a boulder as high as my shoulder, tugged and ripped it from its bed in the sand, sending it crashing over others. Then another. I kept going, scattering rocks and debris around me like a giant insect digging its hole in the sand.

A golden doorway appeared and on its jambs images of the goddess wearing her crown, shaped like a mansion and beside it her titles.

Holy Nephthys, Lady of the Body, Lady of Heaven,
Mistress of the Gods, the Great Goddess...

"The House of Eternity of Nephthys," Harka said in awe. "Great sister of Isis."

"Yes, the dark, morbid one, just as Isis is the light. A goddess to be feared, not just a weaver of linen wrappings, but a weaver of magic. Her tomb will have defences to protect it from the profane. You stay here on guard since you have no light for the darkness."

The priestly keeper did not hide a look of relief following my warnings about the goddess, but Thoth was not to be left behind. He swarmed up my arm and perched on my shoulder, chattering.

I broke open the seal of clay and swung open the gilded leaves of a doorway.

The odour of divinity struck my nostrils.

Again I heard the mournful cry of the kite.

In the resurrection of Osiris, the sisters Isis and Nepthys, stood at either end of the bier over the re-assembled body of the dead god, Nephthys at his head and Isis as his feet, and they were often depicted as two kites, and at other times as women with falcon's wings outstretched protectively.

This was a divine tomb and I could expect divine dangers.

I entered a hallway.

In the glow of my vision, I saw a relief on a wall showing the two sisters. They were crouching on the ground, linen sheath dresses drawn over their knees, bent over an ancient horizontal loom used in the making of linen cloth.

The Two Weavers.

Weavers of magic.

The monkey gave a murmur in my ear.

"Beware, My Master, the windings of Nephthys that enfold the body can also entrap. You do not know what magic she has woven for intruders."

I slowed.

The monkey must have had an inkling of what lay ahead.

We came into a hall, empty it seemed, except for the floor.

"See!"

It was a floor of threads like a spider's web. A giant representation of a loom, countless threads stretching in tension like perspective lines to its length, the warp weighted by a vast drag stone.

A symbol of Nephthys, but this did not represent the cloth of resurrection, I guessed.

A doorway at the end of the chamber led beyond.

I had to cross the flaxen floor to reach it.

Surely the filaments were weak and rotted after thousands of years? The stretched threads were fine enough and would no doubt break as I stepped on them. Yet for safety, I drew my *khopesh* sword from a girdle and armed myself with the protection of its slashing blade.

Protect me, Nephthys.

She did not.

I was only a few steps into the web, when the chamber convulsed and threads engulfed me like a screaming, swirling sandstorm of filaments. The monkey screamed too, clambered down my body and leapt away into the darkness. Wooden rods, pegs, flying shuttles and slashing sticks flew past my eyes and the trap drew my legs tightly and so suddenly that I toppled and now the slashing sticks beat in the strands of thread and jammed me more tightly into the warp and weft of doom.

This was not the cloth of resurrection, but of entrapment, suffocation and death.

The chamber fell silent and I lay bound and helplessly trapped by a million threads.

Now I truly was a Helpless One, I thought.

Had it come to this?

Had I been reborn within the magical threads of Nephthys only to end up trapped in them?

I tried to call out to Harka but wound threads clamped over my mouth like a hand, silencing me.

"I go round about you to protect you, Warrior Hori. I have come to be a protector to you. My strength shall be near you, my strength shall be near you, for ever..."

Forever.

How could I save Egypt now, let alone pursue a forlorn hope of saving Mehyt?

Wrapped in thread and wrapped in hopelessness and silence...

Not quite silence...

I heard chattering.

Thoth came climbing nimbly like a spider along filaments to reach the knotted spindle that was my body.

I saw a flash of shiny bronze.

The monkey had my dagger. Quick thinking, he must have snatched it from my waist as he clambered down my body before leaping into the darkness.

Thoth set to work, gibbering as he slashed, uttering a spell that had been spoken over the dead since time immemorial

"Raise yourself, My Master, throw off your dust, remove the mask which is on your face, loosen your bonds, for they are not bonds, they are the Tresses of Nephthys..."

Nephthys, whose tresses had held me for aeons, had woven me an extra shroud today, one of powerlessness. The ape gave a snickering laugh.

"Did I not warn you of her woven magic?"

"Thank you, wise little one," I said, plucking the last clinging strands from my body. "We are a fighting team as ever."

We went on to the door at the end of the passage and down a long flight of steps to a burial chamber.

Thoth danced on my shoulder.

On a golden catafalque, bordered by four winged images of Nephthys stood an oblong coffin of gold wrapped in enclosed wings.

"Nephthys!"

And at her feet a golden coffer.

Was this the last remaining cache of her bandages of resurrection?

I went closer, knelt, opened its lid.

I released a sigh of wonder at its contents.

Rolls of ancient, yellowing linen torn in narrow strips of bandaging filled the coffer and resting on the sacred cloth a relic even more precious - and potent - than bandages woven by the goddess.

A plaited tress made into a circlet.

And now I recalled the ancient practice of women pulling a front lock of hair in the funeral ritual, and also cutting a piece-lock of hair from the head of professional mourners.

Nephthys was the Mother of all Mourners and so it was natural to conclude that the piece-lock was hers.

Here were the real *Tresses of Nephthys* among the wrappings.

I picked up the plaited circlet in careful fingers, dark and lustrous remnants from the head of the exceedingly beautiful goddess that she had been, the strands still drenched in the perfume of divinity.

I had gained the first cache that Egypt needed to be resurrected.

Now I would have to push back the rocks and cover her tomb when I left so that none should even discover her holy remains.

Lamentations of Isis

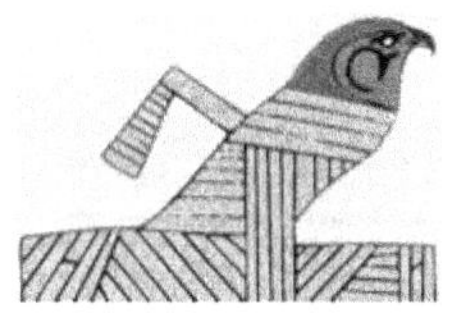

CHAPTER 5

Harka was sitting at the back of the chariot, swinging his legs when I came out.

He jumped down to meet me, relief flooding his face.

He took the golden coffer and stowed it inside the chariot.

"It seems so light to hold the body of a god together."

And to mend a broken land, I thought.

"What is next?"

"Isis. We must gain the Knotted Cords."

"Are we stocking a weaver's shop?"

"So it might seem."

 But we were weaving the destruction of the Hyksos and the rebirth of Egypt.

I set to work covering her tomb with the help of Harka.

Some things had not changed.

I saw farmers guiding wooden ploughs behind their oxen, irrigation worker raising water from the stream in *shadufs,* buckets on long poles pivoted on a fork.

We saw a funeral procession at a distance, servants carrying the tomb owner's goods, sandals, caskets of clothing, chairs and a beds as well and offerings of food and beer in jars, a troupe of female professional mourners piercing the sky with the their ululations of grief, pulling at their front locks and throwing dust on their heads.

Life and death in Egypt.

Passing a grove of palms on the fringes of a farmer's fields, we heard a hubbub on the other side, voices yelling, dogs barking, the crying of women and children.

"What is that disturbance?" I said.

"I can guess. I know that sound. The cry of the oppressed."

"Why?"

"Hyksos tax collectors have arrived. *The hated of heaven.* When the earlier Hyksos kings ruled Egypt they were content to use our administration for their purposes. But King Apophis has taken collection of tax for his treasury into his own rapacious hands. Now, just as the hooves of cattle and donkeys trample the ears of the grain to squeeze the seeds from the husks, the Hyksos crush the farmers under their heels. Instead of taking a one-in-ten share of the crop as of old they demand half, leaving poor families starving."

"Stay here and guard the relic."

I left Harka, who turned the chariot into the shade, and passed through the dimness of palms that rose around me like temple columns.

Coercion in tax collection was as old as Egypt itself. When the scribes and tax collectors arrived, farmers were at their mercy. Farmers who held back their stores of precious food for the year were held down, their backs beaten with rods.

It was expected, an eternal contest between the peasant and the royal purse.

Many a wife of a farmer would berate her husband as a weakling if he yielded too quickly under the beatings and revealed the family's store of hidden grain.

But there was a note of terror and not mere protest in these cries.

I arrived at the edge of the grove to witness a scene of despair in a clearing before a mud-brick house.

A Hyksos official, accompanied by soldiers, had lined up a family - farmer, wife and a string of children. The taxman, in a robe with a shoulder knot, barked at the farmer.

"I will ask you for the last time. Where is your grain, Farmer?"

"It was a poor harvest and yet you came before and took half of our crop, the food from my children's mouths and lo, you have come back again for more. It is unjust and unlawful."

"You want to teach your rulers about law? Then let me teach you about Hyksos farming. While you cut your corn just below the ear with wooden sickles set with flint, we cut below the ear with sickles of sharpened bronze." He made a slicing motion from below his ear to the other side of his flabby neck. He nodded to his soldiers who drew their *khopesh* swords. "Yet we will not begin with the ripened corn, but instead we will harvest the youngest of your crop..."

He pointed to the children.

"Mercy, my Lord," the farmer said, dropping to his knees. "Consider. It is the children who do the gleaning. How then shall we provide for the king?"

The official did not respond to peasant logic.

"Work harder."

"Begin with the lowest sheaf," the taxman said, directing the soldiers to the smallest child at the end of the line.

The hated of heaven.

The farmer's wife set up a shrieking wail in the Egyptian manner.

I had seen enough.

I unslung my bow and set some arrows on a stump beside me, then, putting an arrow to my bowstring, I took aim at a broad Hyksos back as the soldier raised his weapon and the child cowered.

Today I would tax the Hyksos.

With their blood.

I hit the soldier square in the back and followed that arrow with a second.

Another soldier dropped as the third spun around to seek the hidden attacker.

I had the satisfaction of seeing this one's bearded face, his look of surprise as my arrow hit him in the chest.

For the family's sake, I dared not leave a single one of the oppressors alive.

I aimed at the tax collector, going for his heart and hoping my arrow would find one.

When the *hated of heaven* dropped too, I called out from the grove to the farmer.

"Drag the Hyksos carcasses to the river."
Let the Nile carry evidence of my retribution away from the scene.

We stopped to rest and water the horses beside a branch of the Nile in the Delta and let them graze on a patch of grass growing near a grove of palms.
We sat at the river's edge where a breeze stroked the umbels of a papyrus thicket.
The sound reminded me of the whisperings of the dead.
"What happened in the tomb, Great Hori?"
"I, the mummy, ended up being wrapped a second time."
I told him about the attack by the horizontal loom-trap of Nephthys.
His eyes grew round.
The account excited his curiosity about my own wrappings of death.
"Is it fitting to ask how you are bound? Were your wrappings soaked in preservatives and held together with resins and beeswax? Are there magical amulets hidden under the layers?" I was a mystery, like deep and murky water, and once he had dared to toss in a

stone, his curiosity spread like widening ripples. "Did they cut open your side with a stone knife and remove your organs to be stored in canopic jars, also removing your brain with a hook and stuffing your head with cloth to fill the space? Did they lie you to dry in natron for seventy days?"

"What do you think, Harka? That would not leave much of a warrior to defend Egypt."

He looked embarrassed.

"Forgive me."

A child, a little herd boy, came to the river, bringing two spotted cows to drink at the edge.

Fear jumped into his eyes when he saw us sitting nearby, a pair of armed men. Were we the feared oppressors? He saw one man dressed in an Egyptian kilt, though dark like a Nubian and with the shaven head of a priest, and another of indeterminate origin cloaked in a robe and hood like a sand dweller.

"Do not be afraid," I said. "You are among friends. Water your cows."

He gulped, yet went ahead. His cows were thirsty.

As the beasts bent their neck to drink, he kept stealing glances at me with big eyes.

His curiosity overcame him.

"Have you escaped from a tomb, Sir?" he said with the directness of a small child.

"You are observant, Herd Boy, and I cannot lie to you. Yes, I have escaped from the tomb."

He nodded as if this were a perfectly acceptable truth.

Children trusted their eyes, even at the sight of the miraculous and the unbelievable.

"Do you have to go back, or will you stay here?" he said.

"I have to go back. But not yet."

"It is good here."

It was.

My heart went to the boy.

He was Egypt, an Egypt that was still the same after a thousand years of my absence. Eternal Egypt.

Some things would never change.

"It is for such as he that I continue my struggle," I said in a murmur to Harka.

He looked at me as if in a new light.

Perhaps he never expected tenderness from a killer wrapped in the bindings of horror.

I was not looking for her.

I was listening for the whispers of Isis when I heard her.

Mehyt.

Whispering from a tomb.

Not far.

"Hori, my love, tread lightly over my tomb as you pass me by, just as the ages have passed us quietly by…"

Harka noticed the stiffening of my form as he steered the horses across sand between cliffs.

"Danger?"

"No."

"A greater danger than you dare to say," Thoth chattered in my ear. *"Temptation. Block your ears, My Master. You have a mission to revive Egypt. Not your long-dead love Mehyt."*

He was right. I could not stop now.

I had the powerful *Tresses of Nephthys*, yet I needed more and the next cache of talismanic power was even more potent.

"A good decision," Thoth consoled me. *"Perhaps the high god was testing you to see if your love of holy Egypt was greater than your love of a woman."*

We went on quietly and softly over the sleeping earth that hid Mehyt.

I thought of the knotted cord that bound life to death and another invisible cord that tied together those in love, a link that stretched beyond distance or time.

Mehyt had gone long ago to the netherworld, yet her Ka life-force would still be there in the tomb, tied to her body.

It was her Ka that I had heard.

I heard the Kas of all the dead around, but some were distant, a sound no louder than the susurration of reeds in a breeze. Others came to the fore to call to me as Nephthys and now Mehyt had done.

I must listen for Isis, Queen of Heaven, Great of Magic, Egypt's most powerful goddess.

I heard the mournful shriek of a kite in the sky high above.

Isis?

Yes, for now whisperings from a tomb fluttered in my ears.

"You draw near, Hori, who is wrapped in the tresses of my beloved sister... and you bring another precious relic of her... her holy locks of mourning..."

Then, behind her voice, I heard a sound like metallic scraping...

The ragged range of a cliff ended on one side in an edge like great steps, or an empty throne, the symbol of Isis and the shape of her crown.

"She is at the foot of that cliff," I said, pointing.

But as we neared the spot, Harka drew on the reins and turned behind a clump of palms.

Somebody had beaten us to the tomb and they were already at work digging.

We were too late.

Life and death had not changed

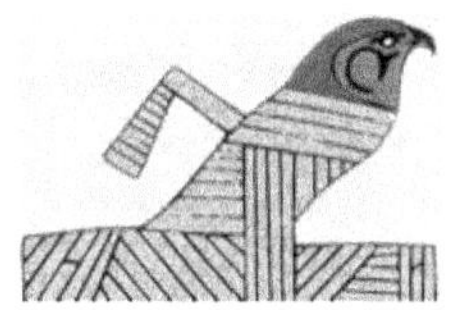

CHAPTER 6

We climbed out of the chariot and crawled closer on the sand.

Harka growled.

"Hyksos, no doubt. Royal-sanctioned tomb robbery. They strip the tombs of our forbears in search of gold for their treasury, extorting the dead as well as the living."

"Not Hyksos," I said, able to make them out clearly. "A gang of Egyptian tomb robbers who feel free enough and desperate enough to loot in this time of Egypt's breakdown."

"What do we do?"

By way of reply, I rose and removed my hooded cloak, the monkey climbing down.

"In better times they would die on pointed stakes for the crime of tomb robbery. Today they may die of fright."

I crept soundlessly behind them.

"Do we have to move a mountain?" one of the gang gave a whispered grumble as he hauled aside a rock. "How can we be sure that a great tomb lies here?"

"Because a friend of a friend of a beer-soaked priest of
Osiris told us so."

"Don't mention beer."

"We have only just begun. You need a drink already?"

"No, I need the courage of beer. Did you not hear that
jackal howling in the desert when we set out? There is a
mood about this place as heavy as these cursed rocks."

"There is more than a mood here," I said.

A workman, a digging tool in his hands, spun.

At the sight of me, he dropped his tool, gasped.

Others turned - and turned into stone.

I stood before them, bare in my wrappings, only part of
my face and eyes visible. I raised my arms, my fingers
clawed. I gave a roar that came from the underworld.

"Run for your lives, desecrators. If you ever dare to
return to this place I will follow you and kill you and all
who know you."

In a short time I found myself alone.

Harka joined me.

We continued the tomb robbers' digging, tearing at the
sand and rocks.

I took a bow, as well as a penetrating battle axe and a sickle sword at my waist.

"Wait here and guard the chariot with the Tresses of Nephthys," I said.

"What army do you expect to meet down there?" the priestly keeper said, puzzled.

"The mother of magic will be guarded by underworld guardians. I have an idea what they might be..."

Thoth clambered up my leg and onto my shoulder.

I entered through the broken doorway.

I found myself in a long, high hall with supporting columns cut out of the living stone. Passages ran off from the hall into darkness.

The odour of divinity wafted to me.

There - a rustling sound, not like leaves or reeds, but metallic.

Thoth heard it too.

He gibbered softly.

"Serpents? I do not like scaly serpents, My Master..."

"Not serpents, something else, equally scaly. Wherever Isis wandered in the land in search of the scattered parts of Osiris she was followed by seven guardians."

"The seven scorpions of Isis!"

His chatter came like an introduction as a sinister creature, a vast black scorpion emerged, swiveling at the end of the hall to face us, pincer claws held out to grapple like a wrestler's arms. Those pincers could snap off an arm, but more fearsome still was the tail that cranked up over its back, dangling a poison sting.

I reached for an arrow in my quiver and Thoth clambered around to my back to hang on to my cloak in dread of the monster.

Where to aim?

It had more armour than a score of Hyksos warriors. The mouth plates gaped. I drew swiftly and shot an arrow into the mouth. A screech followed, either from its mouth or from the sound of its plates as they scraped over each other as it made a rush onwards, unharmed.

I sent another arrow into its tail, which thrashed.

But it kept coming.

Thoth shrieked in fear at the approaching din, still not daring to look.

I abandoned the bow.

A slashing scimitar?

Perhaps.

A pincer came grappling and I struck at a joint with the blade. It was like striking metal, but I severed it part way through.

But now another pincer came swinging in like a second enemy closing in for the kill.

I jumped clear of its snapping claw, switched the sickle blade to my left hand and took up the battle axe from my waist.

Thoth shrieked and clambered even lower and I saw why. The scorpion's tail was arcing down to strike.

I made another leap sideways and swung the war axe. I hit the tail that flashed past my shoulder spurting venom from its barb as it hit the tomb floor.

Crash.

The penetrating Hyksos axe crushed the armoured tail like a crab's shell and its life essence oozed out.

I smashed at the head next, sending the attacker into a grinding reversal down the passage, but now two more took its place.

Thoth leapt off, climbing up a pillar to safety.

I had a weapon that worked. I faced the new arrivals, swinging, crushing, splattering shell and releasing ooze, amid the screeching of metal plates.

Another came from a side passage just as a scorpion struck with its tail.

I twisted away. The spearing barb struck a fellow scorpion instead and it writhed, flashing its tail wildly in every direction. It started a chain reaction as more scorpions tried to clamber over the top of the wounded ones to reach me.

They were killing each other and those they missed, I slew with a rain of axe blows...

Thoth climbed down.

We moved on through the tomb to an oval burial chamber. I saw now that the layout of the tomb with its twisting side passages had been designed in the design of a *Tjet* buckle of Isis.

We reached a doorway, blocked by a writhing curtain.

"Here are your snakes," I said to Thoth.

Living snakes, plaiting and knotting their scaly lengths, hung down in an echo of the magical Knotted Cords of Isis.

I switched to the curved Hyksos blades, but perhaps the serpents of the darkness had seen enough and they dropped down. They slithered into the gloom.

We entered the burial chamber of Isis, Queen of Heaven and Great of Magic. A force like an invisible curtain resisted my body as I approached her golden coffin that echoed the shape of her tomb, a great knot of Isis on its lid and wings of a hawk wrapping around the base.

At her feet sat a coffer of gold.

I opened the coffer.

Divine odour rose to meet my nostrils

And inside, knots of cloth, lengths of it, aged and rusted, twisted in tangles of mystery by the fingers of Isis.

The magical Knotted Cords... and among them amulets to place under the wrappings of the dead.

I now had the *Tresses of Nephthys* and the *Knotted Cords of Isis*. Next I needed to find the Scroll with the magical spells given to Isis by Thoth, which she and Nephthys had used in their chants over the body of Osiris to raise him from the dead.

Then I would have the power to raise and restore a dismembered Egypt.

And more...

A fugitive dream.

I blew on my dream like secret embers to keep them alive. Had I come back to life only to kill, never to love? I closed the coffer and took it up under my arm.

CHAPTER 7

We returned south, the way we had come, the coffers filled with relics at our feet in the chariot.

I heard the whisperings of Mehyt in her tomb, close, thrillingly close.

"O Hori, come to my house!

Long, long have I not seen you.

My heart mourns for you, my eyes seek you,

I search for you to see you!

Come to your beloved, come to your beloved!"

Mehyt was here, in reach, her words like love whispers in my ear from a time long ago as we lay together on a warm night.

I felt a hunger for her arms, then a panic of desire.

Could I once again see the gleam of life in her fine eyes, restore a love that had been severed like Egypt?

I would have to invade her tomb and take her body with me to my sanctuary.

Egypt could wait for a few more hours.

But the words of the High Priest came back to haunt
me.

"How much time do I have?"

*"Precious little. Apophis is searching for the relics,
sending out armed missions from his garrisons, scouring
the land that, as each day goes by, he gains more control
of, guided by a Hyksos priest of Seth named Sutekhy.
You will need all the power you can bring from the
beyond to defeat him. Sutekhy is a magician and a seer,
a scryer of flames, and he will be using his magic to try
to see your every move and to know the secrets of your
heart."*

The ache inside me grew deeper.

How fierce would that ache become if I kept on going,
stretching the distance between us like a rope, growing
in tension, creaking, straining.

Would my heart crumble to dust?

Allowing my mission to fail was unthinkable.

Yet passing Mehyt by and with it the smallest chance of
possessing her again was impossible.

I could face any impossibility to save Egypt, but passing
Mehyt by when she was so near was an impossibility of
the heart that defeated me.

Come! Come! Come!

For though in the tomb I lie,

I will arise and break the bands of Death...

Fragments of a love poem came to me.

"Stop over there," I said to Harka.

The monkey gave a screech. Agitated, it flipped on my shoulder and landed back on its feet.

"My Master," it chattered. *"Hear my words. Your love is not to be found inside the tomb. She is a flower cut and dried, her perfume the scent of an empty jar, the dew of her life gone forever. Will you risk all for a vain heart's desire? I know what you are thinking. You are gathering powers to bring her back. But would you pervert such magic? If any life could spring from such dark enchantment, like a grain seed of corn sprouting briefly in the darkness of a tomb, would it not surely shrink without the will of the gods and the sunlight of divine order? Yes, you are gathering power. But do not choose weakness instead."*

"Stop your chattering, Ape," I said.

Guilt and desire combined to give my voice a roughness that I had never before directed at my long-tailed friend.

Harka caught my mood of grim intent and stopped.

"You seek another relic?"

I did not answer him.

I climbed down from the chariot and began to rip up the earth.

I am coming, Mehyt, I thought. I have not forgotten our vow of long ago.

I tore at the earth and stones.

I broke through an ancient rotted door and moved into the tomb passage when the sound of running footsteps stopped me.

Harka.

"Great Hori, they are coming. Fast. A squadron of chariots and soldiers. I see their dust in the sky."

"Then I will stand and fight them."

"No, you cannot. The relics. We cannot risk them. What if we lose them in a battle? We must go on..."

"Go... go...go!" Thoth shrieked at me.

I swayed in indecision.

I was on the brink of finding Mehyt in her burial chamber.

But when I came out of the tomb I could hear the pounding of hooves and see their dust in the sky.

Even if I ran back and snatched up Mehyt, she could be harmed in a Hyksos attack.

If they destroyed Mehyt, it would rob her of life everlasting, for in our beliefs, without a mummified corpse to return to, the soul would die the second death.

I could not risk that.

I tasted bitter anguish as I ran with Harka to the chariot and we drove the horses on.

"They have our scent. It is as if they are on our trail like hunting dogs," Harka said. "How can that be?"

I knew the reason.

Sutekhy, the dark magician of Seth, had divined our movements in his scrying flames.

We must keep moving.

It was time to return to the sanctuary and prepare for our next great task: to find the *Scroll of Isis* with its spells of resurrection.

"What tomb did we leave behind us, Great Hori?"

I told him about Mehyt.

Harka did not judge me as the monkey had.

"Then your heart is truly alive. If your love is a weakness then it stirs me as much as your might."

We found sanctuary near the city of *On,* site of the once teeming Temple of Ra but now razed by the Hyksos.

Supporters of the High Priest gave us shelter where our horses were fed and watered. This break in our journey would give Harka a chance to rest.

A servant led us to sparely furnished priestly quarters, a cell with a table and grass mats on the stone floor. He brought us food and drink.

Harka tore a conical loaf of bread into pieces and broke the seal on a jar of beer. He offered me bread on a plate.

"For you, Great Hori. You have not eaten in ages. Many ages."

Hori's wit.

"I have no need of food."

"Then beer. You look dry."

"As the desert sand, but no."

"And I suppose you do not have to catch up on missed sleep, either?"

"I have slept too long."

He was hesitant about his next question.

"I have something to ask you, Great Hori," he said. "If I am not too bold."

"Ask."

"When we opened your tomb sanctuary to awaken you, we discovered the usual offerings left behind at your burial to nourish your soul, a haunch of beef, bread, plates of fruit... all dried and withered now. But did your

Ka spirit feed on their essence as our funerary beliefs teach us?"

Harka had a hopeful look in his eyes. He was part-priest and I did not wish to trample on his beliefs.

"Perhaps it is so for some. But they did not sustain me, only comforting the living in the knowledge that they made some sacrifice in my memory."

"And what is it like on the other side? Did you have to overcome animal-headed gatekeepers armed with butchering knives who guarded the doors of night in your path through the underworld? Did they abandon their posts and flee when they saw you coming?"

I hid a smile that Harka's faith in my prowess extended as far as the underworld.

"The demons I saw in the darkness were personal ones I brought to the tomb, tormenting me over things done and most of all, left undone."

"But did you not face the weighing of your soul in the Hall of Judgement? And meet the Lord of the Dead, Osiris, before you were allowed to enter Aaru, the Fields of the Blessed? I ask this to know the truth about the afterlife because I have a sorely-missed brother waiting for me there, a twin, the missing half that I long to be reunited with some day."

"I am sure you will meet him, Harka. But I did not go there, nor did I meet Osiris in his Judgement Hall. There were no weighing scales except my own conscience."

"No Osiris." He swallowed and there was no food or drink in his mouth at the time.

"Not for me. I did not get that far. I was in limbo, in a void, half in this world and the next, half dead and half alive, as I am today."

He fell silent.

While he slept on a mat, snoring after his beer, I paced the cell through the night hours and thought of what could have been and what I had still to do.

The city of *On* was the home of the High Priest and this visit would be an opportunity to make contact and report on our progress.

In the morning, Harka volunteered to be my emissary.

"It is better that I go and you stay hidden with the relics. Your appearance in the city could alarm the population. I will go to the High Priest's house and give him the news of your victories."

The Sethian creature

CHAPTER 8

Why had I become the chosen one to become the undying Defender of Egypt?

As I waited in that tomb-like cell, memories of my life crept back into my mind, and also the memory of my death.

My adoptive mother Henet and soldier father Ibana had whispered to me as a child that I was the last of the strain of Horus, the last of a semi-divine line of Keepers of Egypt and I was handed a sword and a bow even before the snipping of my side-lock of youth in the ceremony of *sebi* at the age of eleven years.

I was trained from dawn to dusk by the Secret Followers of Horus to defend Egypt from its enemies and by flame light at night by priests to write and read the sacred word so that I could understand the heritage that I protected.

The Followers of Horus prepared me for my battles against the demon demigods who had snatched the sceptre of Egypt from the faltering hands of humankind upon the death of the gods.

When I was ready, I fought the demon demigods over the length of Egypt until that day when I met their leader, the Last Son of Seth, the devil god.

I met him in a final battle of men and demigods as they swept south to take the City of the Falcon in Upper Egypt.

We held them off for two days, resisting their demonically powered onslaught until only two were left alive on the bloodied sand of the battlefield, the Son of Seth and I.

The blood of Horus and the blood of the great Usurper faced each other.

"A fitting meeting, Orphan of Horus-seed," he said, his growl emitted from a hook-snouted animal's head.

He was a demon with powers beyond his bloodied sword.

I saw proof of that now as my adoptive father, the soldier Ibana, appeared at my side to give me a cry of warning.

"Flee, Hori, for you must die in this contest."

But old Ibana was long dead and this just a conjuring by the demon who took advantage of my momentary distraction.

He used his shield to ram me to the ground.

Then he swooped with the sword and plunged it into me.

With the last of my metal, tempered by the years of relentless training, I thrust back.

"If die I must in this contest, then so must you."

My sword pierced his belly and I twisted it.

The reign of the demon demigods ended that day.

I was the saviour of Egypt.

Yet I was dead.

Inside the priestly cell, I circled the two coffers filled with the relics of Nephthys and Isis, my thoughts deep and dark.

Instruments of resurrection.

When added to the *Scroll of Isis* they would have a power unimaginable.

I recalled the moment when the High Priest rested a sympathetic hand on my shoulder.

"When Isis and Nephthys raised Osiris it was only for a brief time before he ascended to his kingship of the afterlife. So it is with you. You have risen for a time, Hori,

but your life cannot be prolonged indefinitely and you must return to your rest in the tomb."

"Then my survival is a curse."

A dangerous idea slid into my thoughts like a snake. Once I had gathered together the combined power of the relics, could I bring life - *full life* - not only to Mehyt but also to myself, shedding these wrappings of death to regain a life of human touch and joy?

It was a prompting from the darkness, whisperings from the great serpent that had swallowed the sun of Egypt.

"Leave me, serpent!" I said.

Harka returned with a shadow in his eyes.

"Ra-Hotep sends his praises and gratitude for your achievements and he wishes to meet us in Abydos when we have secured the final relic of the scroll. But I also bring you disturbing news, Great Hori. The Hyksos king in Avaris has sent out emissaries today with an obscure and twisted demand just as he sent his puzzling demand to Pharaoh Seqenenre Tao about the noisy hippos in a canal far across Egypt."

"What message?"

"About the weather, it would seem. But the meaning is hidden. His messengers tell the people:

"Nights can grow cold in Avaris at the edge of the eastern desert. But the fire of a woman's body burning in the night can warm a king's palace. Bring what the king desires within three days, or she will burn in the flames of extinction."

Mehyt.

The message was vague, as twisted as the serpent king who sent it, but the meaning unmistakable.

Apophis had Mehyt and was threatening to set her mummy aflame.

I had left Mehyt's tomb open. The squadron of Hyksos attackers had come upon it and noticed signs of my entry. They had gone inside, found her mummy and carried her off to Avaris.

But why?

Why take the mummy of a Chantress of Ra?

Sutekhy the seer must have divined our ancient love and now the Hyksos king was using the eternal survival of her soul as a sword against me.

I cursed the Hyksos, raged like a panther of the south. I had brought this upon her, brought the threat of eternal peril when I hoped to bring her eternal life.

"The king will destroy Mehyt unless I give them the relics," I said to Harka.

My voice was a groan like one just awakened from the dead.

"You cannot."

"Then I will get her back."

"You cannot."

"I will go to Avaris to rescue her."

"You cannot."

"Do you not have anything useful to say?"

"Avaris is the stronghold capital of Apophis. A high walled fortress bristling with Hyksos soldiers."

"A great city must lie on the river.

"Yes, it does, a harbor city built on a Delta branch of the Nile. Vast enough to berth three hundred ships. But -"

"Then I will go by river."

"Every vessel is searched by Hyksos officials. Believe me, Great Hori, no living thing can get in there."

"Then what about a dead one?"

I told him of my plan.

He marveled greatly.

"But what of the relics? We cannot take them with us into the enemy's lair."

"No. We leave them here with our allies in *On* for safekeeping until our return. We will collect them on the journey back."

Funerary barque

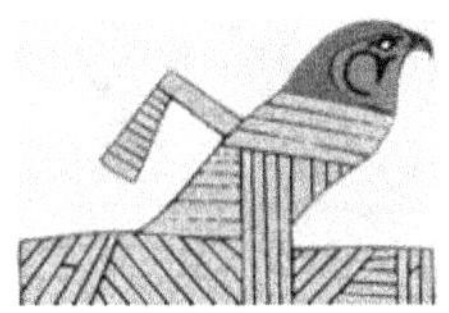

CHAPTER 9

A funerary barque, swept up in papyriform shape at stem and stern, and drawn by a small boat under sail, crewed by sailors loyal to the Ra Priesthood, crept into the harbor of Avaris beneath the towering city stronghold.

Few looked at the new arrival.

The authorities had the living to attend to, arrivals and departures of merchant ships going to the Levant and the island of the Minoans, cargo vessels with goods, tribute and stone from the south.

And this was a funerary boat, a body in a mummy case lying under a shaded canopy and officiated over by a shaven, dark skinned priest.

I looked up through the eyeholes of the mummy case at the soaring walls of Avaris.

Our store of weapons lay hidden beneath me under a false base-board in the mummy case.

But Hyksos eyes had noticed us. As we berthed, a bearded official in an Asiatic cloak with a shoulder knot and a soldier armed with a spear boarded our funerary barque.

"Where is your manifest?"

The Hyksos had ruled Egypt for almost one hundred years and they spoke Egyptian.

"Manifestly we have none," Harka the shaven priest said. "Just the dead body of a pilgrim. In case you Asiatics don't know, every Egyptian is supposed to make a post mortem pilgrimage to Abydos, the home of the god of the dead."

"I know your Egyptian practices. Morbid. Behind our backs you call us barbarians, but we do not mummify our dead like dried fish."

"And we do not bury donkeys and horses with our dead as you Hyksos do, nor sacrifice living servants to accompany dead rulers."

"I have no time to debate comparative religion with you, priest. Open up that box of dried fish for inspection for I have seen devious pilgrims fill these painted boxes with taxable goods instead of their dead."

"You would desecrate a pilgrim's coffin?"

"Open it."

I, along with the bandaged monkey, heard our friend Harka grumble as he opened the coffin, letting in hot air as well as the scents of a city and a busy harbour, wood smoke, baking bread, sour beer, ripening fruit and vegetable, the produce of Egypt and spices from lands afar.

"Hideous," the official said, shuddering. "A dead man and his ape. You Egyptians..."

We waited for darkness before slipping through the wharf storehouses into the city.

We had penetrated the stronghold of the Hyksos.

"While this is the capital of the Asiatics," Harka said, "many Egyptians live here and serve them willingly while others resist them in secret. I have allies who can help our plans."

"We must stay hidden. I plan to make my assault on the palace walls under the cover of darkness."

"The walls are high."

"No wall is high enough to stop Thoth clambering up it with a rope while you keep guard below."

On silent, clothed soles I went like a ghost through the dim corridors of the Asiatic king's palace.

It was a gaudy place with hangings of bright cloth on the walls.

The Asiatics had built a palace, yet made it feel like a desert tent.

The whispering of Mehyt drew me to a chamber, the entrance barred by a guard armed with a spear.

I padded silently to his side and before he had barely twisted his head I grabbed it in my hands had twisted it further.

I stepped over him into a chamber.

In the light of a flaming torch on a wall, I saw a form lying on a dais, a small figure wrapped in a tight outer shroud of yellowed linen.

Mehyt.

My heart leapt towards her as I approached to snatch her up and then my heart gave a kick of surprise as a voice spoke.

"My seer cannot see everything, sadly, but he saw you coming to Avaris, Creature of the Egyptian shadows..."

I did not expect to find the king of the Hyksos contemplating his trophy at night.

"You have what is mine," I said.

"And you have what should be mine." He stepped into the flame light - more, went directly to it, taking the torch from the wall.

He took the crackling flame to the edge of Mehyt's shroud.

I saw that he had a dagger at his side.

Monkey slipped unseen down my body. He disappeared like a puff of grey smoke into the chamber's shadows.

"Shall we warm ourselves?"Apophis said. "I had thought you might bring my prizes to Avaris, but no, it seems…" There was something of the reptile about the tight, lipless mouth inside a beard and the black, unblinking stare. The king wore a coloured robe spurning the purity of whiteness that distinguished Egyptians. And worse, he wore a king's robe of unclean wool that Egyptians abhorred.

"Strange," he said, "that the Egyptians would choose a spectre of death and decay such as you to try to revive their hope of freedom." The voice that came out of the black beard was a warning slither. "But it is a dying hope, just as Seqenenre Tao found out, his head smashed like an eggshell in the battlefield. You were outclassed and overpowered, as you should have been, for Egypt's time in the sun is over. For all your pyramids, temples and vain colossi you are a stagnant, dead civilization like this mummified woman here, bound by the dryness of her cloth as Egypt is bounded by dry deserts - borders that Egypt thought would protect it from invaders forever. But the world has changed and your static race has failed to change with it."

He moved the torch to the foot of the shroud.

I knew how the bodies of the dead could burn, blasted dry in natron over seventy days and then drenched in flammable oils and spices in their Night of Ointment and Bandages.

One lick from that flame would be like lighting the wick of a lamp that would quickly leap into a blaze of destruction.

'Oh Mehyt, what peril I have brought you to...' I thought.

"Don't," I said.

"No? Can't you feel that chill in the night air, Egyptian? Ah, but you are well wrapped." He glanced down at the mummy of Mehyt. "You two make a pair. The great love of your life looks pathetically small in her wrappings, don't you think? She will quickly reduce to ashes, yet her fire will warm me for a time."

"Burn her and you will die."

"We all die. Well, most of us. And I was rather hoping I could avoid death myself once I had the Secrets of Osiris in my hands and the powers of resurrection at my command. Say goodnight to your old flame..."

"I will lead you to the relics. I have gathered them in a hiding place."

"So my seer has told me, but he has been unable to see exactly where that hiding place may be. Perhaps hidden in some sanctuary protected by barriers of ancient magic?"

"Stop!"

"I suppose you would promise me anything at this moment, but would you really mean it? Would you not try to trick me later, once I took the flame away?"

"I will tell you exactly where to find the relics. You have nothing to lose."

"I am listening, but the promise of warmth from these burning wrappings is calling."

He moved closer.

Sparks spat out from the torch, landing on the outer shroud. Any one of those pinpoint spurts of light could ignite her dry cloth.

"Am I convincing you that your battle is over, Hori the Mummy?" he said.

I had to stop him, but I was powerless.

Yet a small scampering creature was not.

The puff of grey, trailing its long tail, leapt onto his foot, sinking its sharp fangs into a toe.

The Hyksos King gave a bellow of pain.

The torch flew out of his hand, falling on him to ignite his woolen robe in flames.

"Guards! Guards!"

Apophis, beating the flames on his robe now singeing his beard and hair, fled to the door.

I doused a spark on the foot of Mehyt's shroud before snatching her up.

She was light as a husk under my arm and the words of the monkey rang again in my ears...

She is a flower cut and dried, her perfume the scent of an empty jar, the dew of her life gone forever.

I ran with her body, following the darkened corridors of the Hyksos palace and found my way out into the blackness of a courtyard.

I did not lack cloth and I slung Mehyt to myself in a loop of it, bearing her on my back as I climbed the rope, just as the dead were often depicted riding on the back of a bull into the underworld.

At dawn a funerary barque set off from Avaris on its journey of pilgrimage towards Abydos, the resting place of Osiris.

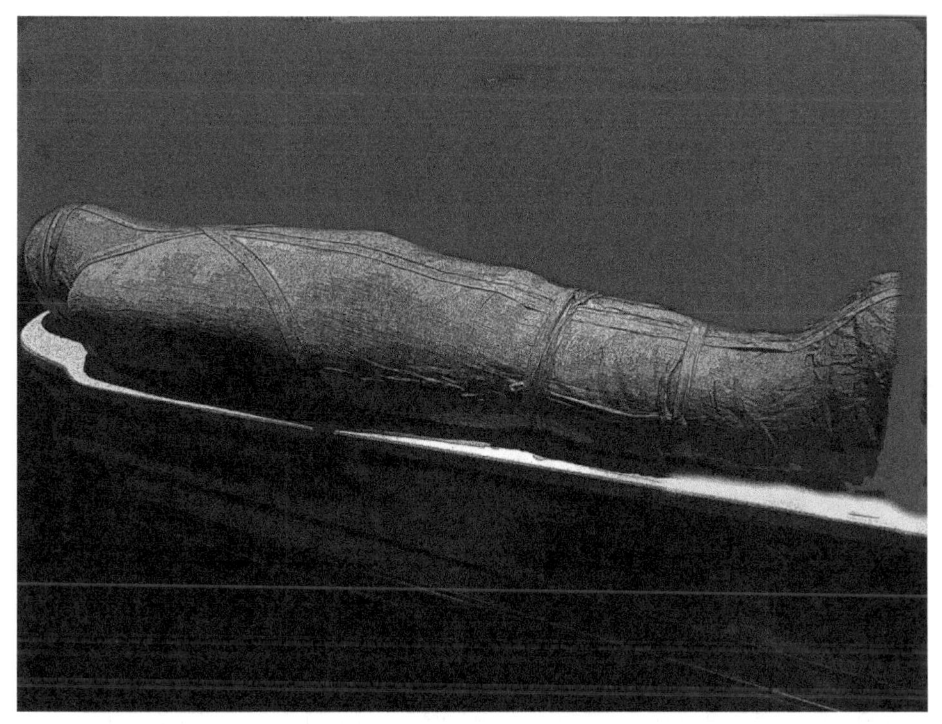

Mehyt

CHAPTER 10

I had Mehyt again.

Or at least a fragrant husk of what held my beloved, the cut and dried flower of what had once been a paragon of vibrant, loving womanhood.

She lay secure in the coffin on the funerary barque, after we had removed our hidden weapons under the false base-board.

All that remained to be found was the *Scroll of Isis*, then I could think about taking the terrible step of defying the laws of Maat, committing the crime of rejecting the divine order of existence.

But first I needed the scroll.

We sailed along the branch of the Nile under a southern breeze and into the widening river, journeying upstream to the Nome of Thoth, pausing briefly on the way at the city of *On* to collect the relics that had been kept with allies.

I hid them for safety inside the coffin.

We passed barges heavy with cut stone, slow moving traders, and Hyksos fighting ships loaded with the army of Apophis redeploying after the battle against Seqenenre Tao.

Egypt was under occupation, the once proud land trapped by Asiatics in the North and an ancient foe beyond our far Southern border, the warlike bowmen of Nubia.

I dreaded the possibility of the two ever coming together, forming an alliance to complete the dismemberment of Egypt between them.

Apophis must be stopped before that.

The Hyksos wave had spread to the Nome of Thoth we learnt when we reached the city of *Khemenu,* near the boundary between Lower and Upper Egypt.

The monkey jumped on the prow and chattered excitedly as the pylons of the great stone temple of Thoth rose like a fortress of learning above the palm-lined river for this was the home of the god Thoth, Lord of writing and magic and site of his secret libraries of forbidden knowledge.

My little ape was visiting his spiritual home.

We arrived to find a Hyksos vessel, a Byblos boat, moored at the wharf and learnt that under the orders of king Apophis an armed Hyksos mission was systematically looting the Nome of its sacred writings.

Ashore, Harka sent word for allies.
An old man from the temple of Thoth, Djehutymose, a temple Keeper of Scrolls, came to meet with us.
He sat with us on the floor of the tow-boat's deckhouse
The librarian was a wise little man in pleated robes as white as an ibis.
He blanched as he looked at my face inside the hooded cowl.
"I see one here with us who sits on the wrong side of the gates of death."
"This is the Great Hori," Harka introduced me in a tone of respect. "Egypt's Ancient Defender, as oracles foretold."
"And this is his little ape, I see. Hello, monkey. By his wrappings, it would seem that he has escaped from our animal necropolis!"
Thoth took no offence at this, greeting him like an old friend.

It was the first time I ever saw the little ape clamber
onto a stranger's shoulder

He murmured in the man's ear.

The librarian gave a bird-like cackle.

"He tickles my ears with a monkey joke and I am in
need of cheering this day. Woe is the city of *Khemenu*,
my friends, woe is Egypt! My library is turned upside
down and I am banished from the precinct. The Hyksos
have sacked our repository of sacred writings."

"Taken all?"

"Not all. They have traitors advising them and they seem
to know what they are looking for. Scrolls of forbidden
power which they are loading on their vessel in the
harbour."

"Then we are too late," I said in a dead voice.

Apophis had beaten us. I had failed in the final mission.

"Too late for what?" Djehuty said.

"For the scroll we have come here to seek. The Secret of
Isis, a scroll containing the resurrection spells that Isis
and Nephthys used to resurrect the god Osiris."

"A scroll far too precious to sit round in a temple. The
greatest funerary document in history was buried."

"Then they may not have found it?"

"I cannot say. They are digging up *Khemenu* in their ruthless search, even digging beneath the stone baboon colossi that sit in front of our temple of Thoth."

"Where would the scroll be buried?"

"Inside a place that would disturb your little monkey friend, I fear. The vast hidden animal necropolis of ape and ibis mummies in the desert outside the city."

Rows of ancient withered apes, their rotting bandages unspooling around their bodies, stared out at us from alcoves in the honeycomb of tombs.

I had left Harka behind to guard the relics and given him orders to sail with the relics to the safety of my sanctuary if I did not return.

The Keeper of Scrolls lit the way with a flaming torch. Little Thoth was no stranger to death, yet the thronged millions of his dead cousins threw him into clinging silence.

Beyond the ape catacomb we entered an ibis catacomb, an underground sanctuary stocked with millions of desiccated birds, each one crammed into its own separate jar, the mouth sealed with plaster.

After many twists and turns in a bewildering labyrinth of passages we arrived a doorway and the sight of a smashed wooden and copper lined gate.

"This is bad sign."

The Hyksos raiders had been here.

A glance inside at the slag-heap of crumbled yellow scrolls and dashed clay pots used to house the writings confirmed his fears.

"They have taken it."

"How can you be sure? Look, there are scrolls scattered everywhere," I said, though my hopes had been overturned like this chamber. "It could be any of these."

"No, it could not." He was adamant. "Trust me, I am a Keeper of the Scrolls. I know the scroll in question and I believe they did too. They would have recognised it from its container once they dug their way through the alcoves. The Scroll was housed in a blood red jar, you see, like the red jasper Buckle of Isis... "

"Where is it now?"

He shrugged.

"Loaded onto their vessel along with the rest of the stolen writings to be transported to Avaris, I assume."

"When do they sail?"

"This day, according to word at the docks."

"Then I must hurry."

"You plan to stop a Hyksos boat?"

"Yes."

"And then"

"Take it back. If I am not too late."

The god Thoth as a baboon

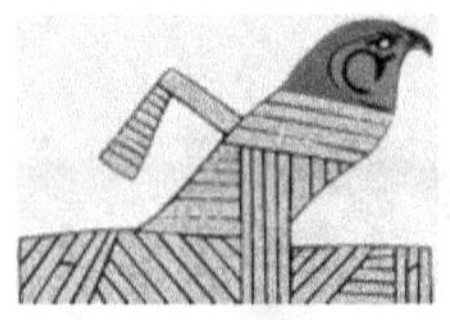

CHAPTER 11

I was too late.

I returned to our boat to be greeted by the sight of the Biblos boat with its square sail unfurled, slipping gently downstream on its journey to the stronghold of Avaris.

"They have the scroll on board," I told Harka. "We are too late."

They had the scroll aboard a Hyksos vessel under sail and we had a funerary barque tied to a sailboat.

Yet the Byblos boat was a sea going vessel, slow and cumbersome.

Our smaller boat was a river craft, faster, more nimble and with the aid of the current we might surprise them.

Speed could be our advantage.

Speed and the help of a funerary barque.

I explained my plan to Harka and the small crew of our tow-boat.

They murmured among themselves, but were too intimidated by the sight of me to argue.

"He is the Great Hori," Harka assured them. "He could overpower the Hyksos fleet."

"I may need a little help," I said, breaking out the weapons hidden beneath the coffin and handing them out, keeping a war axe for myself which I slung from my waist.

We set sail in pursuit.

It seemed a forlorn hope at first as the gap between us grew, but out in a current and clawing the breeze with our sail, we began to speed after them like a water beetle.

We had no need to disguise our pursuit, I reasoned. The Hyksos would hardly be alarmed to find themselves chased down by water-borne cortege.

When they spotted us closing on them they laughed.

"Why bring your dead to the Delta? Leave them on the battlefield where they fell like flies!"

"Are you racing us?" a crewman yelled at us. "Or is there an underworld demon chasing your dead?"

We caught them, our boat passing to their bow and the funerary barque drawing beside them.

They never guessed that death was about to overtake them as they gathered, amazed at our impudence at taunting the conquerors.

It was exactly the response I wanted.

None on board the Byblos boat observed me as I slipped out of the boathouse and leaped from our vessel to theirs, cheered on by my monkey climbing up the riggings of the tow-boat.

I fell on the startled Hyksos with my axe, shoving others over the side.

Harka, swinging a *khopesh* sword, and sailors from our tow-boat, joined me in the fight as, too late, the Hyksos discovered that the joke had turned bitter and reached in vain for their weapons.

I slew ten Hyksos that day.

Harka and the sailors accounted for the rest.

I opened a deck hatch and descended a wooden ladder to the boat's hold.

There I found the ruby red jar of Isis among a hoard of jars and scrolls.

I had recovered all three relics.

But now a Hyksos warship appeared ahead, sailing against the current in the river's deeper channel.

I ordered our sailors to lash the rudder of the captured Hyksos vessel, setting it on a collision course.

Then we jumped back on our boat, and continued South, now the most jubilant funeral cortege in Egypt.

We looked back to see the Byblos boat and the warship slam into each other with a splintering of timber, the force toppling their masts.

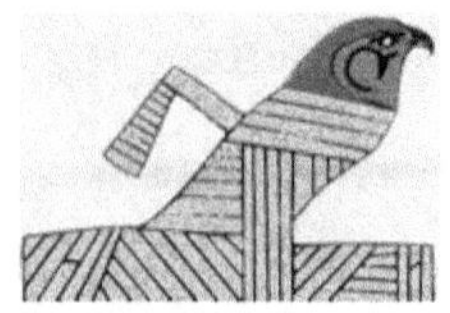

CHAPTER 12

We were safe in my sanctuary and so were the tools of power.

I looked into my soul.

I had risen to defend Egypt from the evil of a foreign enemy, not to regain a love lost.

Using the divine relics for my own ends would be diverting them from their intended purpose, ignoring the solemn commission handed to me by the Prophet of Ra.

Restore Egypt or restore Mehyt?

Do both, a small voice whispered to me, a voice that did not come from the monkey on my shoulder.

The little monkey had a different message for me.

"Do not do it, My Master."

"Get down, Thoth. The time for warnings is over."

I set the two golden coffers beside Mehyt on the slab, as well the *Scroll of Isis.*

The priestly soldier Harka watched on grimly, his dark skin ashen.

He trusted me boundlessly in all things.

But this?

"I cannot attempt this alone," I said.

He was halfway a priest and I was halfway a corpse like Mehyt.

Between the pair of us could we somehow awaken the dead?

I heard the far off shriek of kites in the desert beyond my sanctuary.

The spirits of Isis and Nepthys?

Harka took up the aged and flaking *Scroll of Isis*, while I opened the golden coffers.

I began with the *Tresses of Nephthys*.

I took out rolls of the wrapping and draped them on her form, running them from side to side across her body like coffered bandages, beginning at her head and working down to her feet. They were lengths of linen cloth, yet they seemed alive in my hands.

As I worked I paused to slip amulets under the wrappings, first a blood red Buckle of Isis in red jasper, giving the breath of life....

The chamber of the sanctuary seemed be holding its breath.

"Begin the spells," I said.

Harka cleared a tightness in his throat.

He began shakily, a voice filled with dread that slowly gained power and confidence that came from the words themselves.

"The blood of Isis, the incantations of Isis, the power of Isis," Harka intoned. *"Rise up O resting of heart, shine O resting of heart. Raise yourself, Mehyt, throw off your dust, remove the mask which is in your face, loosen your bonds, for they are not bonds, they are the Tresses of Nephthys."*

Then under the wrappings I placed the golden Djed pillar of preservation, stability and eternity, next the jeweled golden heart scarab of resurrection, the two frogs of resurrection and the ankh of eternal life...

I took the plaited circlet of hair and placed it on the head of the shroud.

Next came the magic of *Knotted Cords*. They crackled with life in my hands as I snaked their length over the bandages.

Harka continued:

Arise Helpless One!

Arise Helpless One Asleep!

Arise Helpless One in this place

which you know not; yet I know it!

Behold, I have found you lying on your side

Listless One.

'Ah, Sister!' says Isis to Nephthys,

'This is our daughter Mehyt,

Come, let us raise her head,

Come, let us rejoin her bones,

Come, let us reassemble her limbs,

Come, let us put an end to all her woe,

that, as far as we can help, she will weary no more,

but rise like brother Osiris..."

Now a great gasp arose in the chamber, sucking away the air.

I heard a sobbing like the wind.

Was it the mourning of Isis and Nephthys?

The shroud moved.

Mehyt.

She would need air to breathe.

But as my hands fell on the wrappings above her face to rip away the shroud and yellowed cloth from her face I heard her voice in my head, not as a fluttering like the wind, but this time like the howling of a gale.

"Oh Hori, stop! Is this what you wish? For me? For us? A half life together? I would rather rest in the afterlife with full memories of our life together than this, though I love you as life itself."

My fingers, already hooked to tear and rip, froze above her head.

What had I tried to do?
My heart was dust.
I had found her tomb and rescued her from the stronghold city of Avaris in vain.
She was not to be mine again in flesh and touching warmth but only in distant memory.
Oh, Mehyt.

I could not risk taking her back to her resting place while the forces of Apophis searched for her.
Worse than any tomb robber, I had robbed Mehyt not of her tomb goods, but of her tomb itself, her House of Eternity.
She would have to share my tomb.
I left her shrouded body in my sanctuary and we sailed to Abydos and the tomb of Osiris.
Would my struggles to raise Egypt from the dead be any more successful?

"Her perfume is the scent of an empty jar..."

CHAPTER 13

The dirge-deep voice of Osiris whispering in my ears led us to the cliffs beyond Abydos.

"Hori, Good Servant, you approach me as no other mortal in all of creation, as a dweller in two realms, death and life. Who will judge your soul at the end of time?"

This time I came not only with Thoth and Harka, but with Ra-Hotep, the High Priest of Ra, a procession of his priests, one wearing the mask of Anubis, armed temple guards, and two priestesses wearing golden masks of kites on their faces, assuming the roles of the mourning sisters Isis and Nephthys.

Ceremonies reenacting the drama of Osiris and his death and resurrection were celebrated each year on the processional road across the plain of Abydos, but never before had priests come to symbolically raise Egypt itself.

The High Priest of Ra in priestly robes and collar, his skin dusted with gold, spoke to me as we walked.

"You have risen, Hori, not just as a fighter and Defender of Egypt, but risen to this mighty challenge set before you. You have secured the Secret of Osiris, finding the relics of Egypt while denying king Apophis his dark desires. Tonight will be the apotheosis of Ra's spiritual struggle against the darkness of The Great Serpent. The rites we enact tonight will set in motion mighty forces that will begin the liberation of Egypt from its foreign oppressors, strengthening the arm of the successors of Seqenenre Tao - Kamose and young Ahmose - the new hope of Egypt. You have done well."

But I thought only of Mehyt and how my vain digression from my mission might have brought all of this undone. The priest went on.

"Ra's oracles have told that in the far future other conquerors and other empires will come and try to wrest the forbidden secrets and treasures from mother Egypt, but you will be there, for all time, ready to be raised again like a hidden sword."

Tearing away rocks and scree and helped by the priests, I revealed the staircase of the god and we went down it, the procession bearing torches into an underworld where a peculiar blue mist with the odour of incense-smoke filled the darkness.

We had entered a vast void beneath the cliffs.

"The Mansion of Osiris," the High Priest announced as we arrived at pylon gates. Not for the god of the underworld a House of Eternity, but rather a mansion that was as much an underground fortress.

What defences would the death god Osiris have in place to guard his rest?

Or would Osiris welcome us as the just ruler of the underworld and the judge of souls?

"We shall come to no harm here," the High Priest of Ra said.

We arrived at a hall like a tableau of the underworld, where a vast set of scales stood with two golden weighing pans and the images of the 42 judges of the dead lining the walls, bearded gods sitting with their knees upraised in tight robes.

In the firelight, they seemed alive, their dark eyes, wide in their whites, observing our arrival.

In another scene stood Ammit, the Great Devourer of Souls and Eater of Hearts, who devoured the souls of any who failed the trial of the scales, a nightmarish hybrid with the scaly jaws of a crocodile, the

forequarters of a lion and the hind quarters of a
hippopotamus.

The hippopotamus put me in mind of the Hyksos King
and his twisted demands to Seqenenre Tao.

Were the king's forces, guided by the seer, sniffing on
our trail like graveyard jackals?

We found the stone sarcophagus of Osiris in pure,
glowing white alabaster lying at the top of a long flight of
stairs like a staircase to the heavens and climbed to
meet him.

Here the ceremony could begin.

Within a ring of torch flames held by the priests, the
goddesses Isis and Nephthys, in the form of two
priestesses wearing the golden mask of kites, took their
positions at either end of his bier, while the High Priest
unrolled the scroll.

Two long, startling shrieks pierced the darkness with an
ominous sound that turned the blood to dust, the
keening of unseen birds that flitted about the cavern
spaces

"The two screechers are here," Ra-Hotep said, "and they
are the sisters of Osiris, Isis and Nephthys."

Thoth gibbered nervously in my ear.

I could not tear my eyes away from the white
sarcophagus that shed a milky radiance of power.

Here lay Osiris, the man-god who crossed from life to death and back again giving Egyptians the hope of survival.

Father of Horus, progenitor of the Horus line of which I was the last to survive.

Ra-Hotep began by addressing Osiris in a voice of power that shook with reverence:

"O Great God, Lord of Abydos, we call on you in the presence of the Two Sisters in your house of Osiris-Khentamenti.

Glorify your soul! Praise to your spirit! Breath to your nostrils and to your parched throat!

Give gladness to the heart of Isis and to that of Nephthys, the Two Weepers who bring you the Tresses of Nephthys and the Knotted Cord of life..."

The black jackal-headed priest dressed as Anubis, Lord of the Cemetery, unwound the wrappings of Nephthys, draping the body of Osiris as I had done with Mehyt, lacing the bandaging from side to side in a coffered pattern, pausing to slide the amulets of Isis underneath, starting with the ruby Buckle of Isis in red jasper, the breath of life....

"The blood of Isis, the incantations of Isis, the power of Isis," the High Priest chanted. *"Rise up, O Egypt, resting of heart, shine, O resting of heart. Raise yourself, Egypt,*

throw off your dust, remove the mask which is in your face, loosen your bonds, for they are not bonds, they are the tresses of Nephthys."

Next Anubis took out the plaited circlet of hair from the coffer of gold and placed it at the head of the sarcophagus.

"The Tresses of Nephthys!"

Ra-Hotep chanted:

Ah Helpless One!

You rise for us like Ra every day,

You shine for us like Atum,

Gods and men live by your sight.

As you rise for us you light the Two Lands,

The Land of light is filled with your presence;

You are the body of Egypt,

The fertile Black Soil, rising and dying like the great cycle of the planting and harvesting of corn.

Your body was broken on the threshing floor.

But your seed was planted and with the inundation your bounteousness sprang forth again.

Ah Helpless One Asleep!

Ah Helpless One in this place

In a land you no longer know.

Behold, we have found you lying on your side, Listless

One."

The goddess Isis now spoke:

"Ah, Sister!"' she called across to Nephthys. "This body is the benighted land of Egypt, under the foreign heel of the vile Asiatic.

The sun has been swallowed by the serpent..."

The priest picked up the text:

"Come, let us raise Egypt's head,

Come, let us rejoin Egypt' bones,

Come, let us reassemble Egypt's limbs,

Come, let us put an end to all her woe, that, as far as we can help, Egypt will weary no more, but rise like Osiris..."

Now a darting shadow of a bird flew out of the darkness. It circled our firelight, giving great cries of keening, sobbing, mourning, howling like the wind.

"Winged Isis."

Her flying circle closed and we soon felt the wind of her beating wings and the circle of flames twisted in the hands of the priests.

The hawk shadow landed, settling over the loins of the coffin.

"Isis has reunited with Osiris to bring forth the golden Horus of a new Egypt!" Ra-Hotep said in an ecstatic cry.

But now another cry caught our ears, a warning cry from below the stairs.

"The Mansions of Osiris are under attack. The forces of king Apophis have arrived with a legion of chariots and the entrance has already fallen…"

"Too late. It is done," Ra-Hotep said. "The serpent is too late."

"Is he?" I said. "Or can he still snatch victory? What if the Mansion falls and he seizes the precious relics of power?"

"That cannot happen!" The rapture drained from his face. "With the relics, his magicians could work reverse magic."

"Then we must fight," I said. "Defend the pylon entrance," I ordered the priestly guards. "Harka, take charge. I will climb the pylon roof with my bow and try to stop their advance."

The Hyksos, carrying flames, broke into the cavern led by swordsmen with shields.

I looked down from my position above a pylon, as I searched for a target.

There, an exposed shoulder.

The monkey jumped down as I stretched the bow and snapped an arrow from the string. A soldier spun back, knocking the shield from another and giving me a second target. I hit him in the throat.

I saw a leader wearing a bronze mask of the god Seth point up at me and heard a warning cry from the mask like the blast of a brazen trumpet. Enemy archers unslung their bows and snatched arrows from their quivers. They returned fire, while soldiers rushed the pylon gates.

I ducked a swarm of whistling shafts, nocked another arrow to my bowstring.

When I raised my head the Sethian leader was gone and I heard the clash at the gates as Hyksos surged forward.

The Mansion of Osiris was falling.

I slid the bow over my shoulder and grasped the handle of my *khopesh,* running to the stone steps that linked the roof with a courtyard.

But I did not reach them.

The monkey screeched a warning.

The Sethian, armed with a battle axe, had climbed the pylon to meet me.

His bulk blocked my way.

Flames from below lit a brazen animal's head with long, erect, and square-tipped ears and the hooked snout of a fabulous hybrid beast, part pig, part oryx, part donkey, part ant-eater.

The magician Sutekhy challenged me, an evil spectre in his mask of the warrior devil-god Seth.

"I have longed to meet Egypt's champion," the Hyksos said in a rattle through the snout of his mask. "Egypt could not find a living defender so it has found a dead one instead. And you are already wrapped for burial. But first a swift and final death."

Sutekhy would bring animal strength and guile to this combat, I thought.

And an invisible weapon.

Magic.

"Hori!"

A woman's voice.

One I knew and had not forgotten in centuries.

It ripped me around.

I gaped at the female figure that came into the enemy's firelight glow washing up from below.

It was Mehyt, risen from her wrappings.

How did she come to be here?

Had I begun a process of revivification in the tomb sanctuary that could not be halted?

Had Mehyt risen and come after me?

While these thoughts pinned me to the roof of the pylon, Sutekhy used the distraction to strike the sword from my hands. It hit the stone with a crash and tinkle of shattered bronze.

Sutekhy had me, and more dangerously, my mind, at his mercy.

He had used the weapon of my own heart against me just as the Son of Seth had done when he took my life in the battlefield ages before, invoking the image of Ibana my adoptive father.

Mehyt faded into the darkness like a ghost departing, but the hope that had sprung up in my heart at seeing her arisen remained.

Was she alive inside the sanctuary, weak from her rising, unable to crawl out of the tomb and reach the restoring power of the sunlight?

The solar priests had angled copper mirrors to flash sunlight from the world above to the place where I lay in the earth.

Mehyt would be in darkness. Without that beneficent warmth of the sun would she die again, the second death that every Egyptian feared, without her mummy wrappings and house of eternity?

I saw a movement in the shadows. The monkey made a darting attack on the Sethian creature.

It pounced on the attacker's foot to deliver a bite, but the masked attacker kicked, sending the little creature rolling like a ball.

I shook the ghost of Mehyt from my mind.

CHAPTER 14

He did not hurry.

He had no need.

I had no time to arm the bow.

I was already defeated, confounded by magic and bested at arms.

"In the scripture of your defeated land, Divine Seth cut up the body of Osiris into fourteen pieces. And so I will do the same with you, Bandaged One. How fitting this will be in the very tomb of Osiris. Severing your hands, arms, head, body, legs... There is great symmetry at work tonight, the mark of magic. Your misguided priests have performed a rite of re-enactment, bringing life to Osiris in his embodiment of the land of Egypt. I shall do the reverse to you, cutting up your body like that of Osiris, just as our armies have divided your moribund land. Perhaps I should scatter your pieces across the land as divine Seth did, but you are not worth the effort. I shall be satisfied with a kill, as will our great king,

Apophis, whom you have angered greatly. Die Egyptian, permanently!"

He swung at my head, a sweeping blow to smash it from my shoulders. But a high sweep exposed him below.

I dropped and rolled at his legs like a barrel, sending him tottering back to end up at the very edge of the pylon.

I had time to slip off the bow and nock an arrow.

Bow against axe and body armour and a head covered in a bronze mask.

He dared me to shoot.

I needed a weak spot.

I looked at the hooked mouth.

Unreachable.

The eyes flashing behind the eye-holes dared me instead.

A risky, perilously small target. The arrow leapt.

His hand moved.

My arrow snapped into the wooden handle of his axe.

The Hyksos gave a funneled roar of laughter, snapped off the arrow shaft and tossed it away.

I had only a dagger left, a puny weapon against a battle axe.

Sutekhy came to finish me.

But I remembered that day of practice with Harka when my arrow from a strengthened bow that took a year to make had sent an arrow clean through a bronze shield. The haft of the axe would be weakened, shot through by the arrowhead.

I needed to lure him into striking the pylon stone and it would snap.

I dropped to my knees as if in surrender.

"You are hoping for mercy?"

He swung.

My powers from beyond gave me speed to roll in a blur. His smashing axe-head struck stone with a *clang.* It threw up a shower of sparks as it broke from its handle, the blade whistling over the edge of the pylon.

"No, I was hoping you would do that."

Now, in the moment he would have struck again had he still a weapon in hand, I drove the dagger up under his armour.

The beast toppled.

I, a bandaged avatar of Osiris, had enacted revenge on a murderous son of Seth.

I returned to a scene of carnage.

I climbed body-strewn steps to find a circle of dead,
priestly defenders and Hyksos dead

The pure white alabaster coffin of Osiris lay smashed in
the iconoclastic rage of the Hyksos marauders. The
relics were gone.

The High Priest Ra-Hotep and the golden-masked
priestesses lay stretched out at the dais as if in
swooning obeisance.

I found Harka too, fallen in defence of the pylon gate,
though his sword had taken its toll of Hyksos attackers.

He had always believed in me.

Yet I had failed him in this battle.

King Apophis would have his relics of power to direct
reverse magic against Egypt in some blasphemous rite
in his temple of Seth, even if his chief magician lay
dead.

I came out into darkness.

The Hyksos had paid for their victory.

With a number of dead in the tomb of Osiris, they had
abandoned some chariots.

I chose one drawn by a pair of steeds as white as the
sarcophagus of Osiris.

I would chase them down.

"One man against an army, My Master?" the monkey on
my shoulder chattered.

It reminded me of the first day of my rising when I looked over the heights as the dust of the two armies converged like opposing sandstorms.

Harka, the young priestly soldier lying beside me at the edge said:

"Oh, if only you had been down there in your full strength, Great Hori," the young warrior priest Harka said. "You would have crushed the Hyksos army into the sand."

I flicked the reins over the horses' backs and drove them forward.

I saw them at dawn from the heights.

They were on a plain.

Squadrons of chariots carrying armed Hyksos warriors, an army on the roll.

I spoke to the monkey.

"This will be bloody. Sit on the heights and watch, little Thoth."

"But there are many and you are few."

"Then call on the magic of your namesake Thoth, your animal-headed God of spells who has the head of an ape or of an ibis..."

"Call on animals?"

He chattered in rapid monkey talk that I did not understand and scampered up the highest protruding rock that overlooked the plain.

"If I don't come back, try to find your way back to the sanctuary and see if Mehyt needs help. Maybe you can shine a mirror of sunlight for her or devise some other rescue using your shrewd abilities."

I used the slope to gain speed, drawing momentum as I went into attack.

One chariot stood out, slowing the advance of the army, a chariot holding two armed guards as well as a driver. The carrier of the precious relics, I guessed.

I went at the flank like an arrow from a Hyksos bow. Surprise was my weapon.

Once they saw me they would turn the day to midnight with the flights of their arrows that no attacker or flying horse could withstand.

I heard a far off screech, not of birds, I thought, but of an animal. I flung a glance back and saw little Thoth standing high on his back legs, his arms up as if in a praying gesture to the heavens.

But why the strange screeching call?

I swung back to my target.

I was almost the distance of two Hyksos arrow shots from the chariots, my horses' necks arched like bows, chariot wheels buzzing over sand and ribbons of dust flying behind.

Now one bowshot distance.

I lashed the reins to my waist and put an arrow to my bow, clutching spare arrows in my fingers for immediate use.

I was just in their range when they saw me.

I needed to clear a path to my target. My first arrow hit a driver, but my next missed the warrior as my wheel hit a stone or ridge that jarred the flying platform and threw my aim.

Yet my strike on the Hyksos driver was enough to send their chariot colliding into another, upsetting both in a tangle of whinnying horses and chariots throwing up sand.

A brief victory.

But it had alerted the Hyksos army and a score of bows were raised and turning at me.

Right then the sky darkened, but not with the fletched arrows of the Hyksos, but with squadrons of feathered allies, dense clouds of diving ibis, egrets, eagles, kites, sparrows..

Thoth had called out to nature to save his master.

The day turned to night.

I saw an opening and my target ahead.

The carrier of relics was in my sights.

I removed the bewildered occupants with just three arrows, rode in close to the empty chariot and leapt from mine to the new one.

The bird squadrons circled and dived in relentless attacks, shrieking, keening, screeching, cawing, hooting...

I made for the heights and saw Thoth doing somersaults of delight on his rocky perch.

Thoth was a friend for eternity.

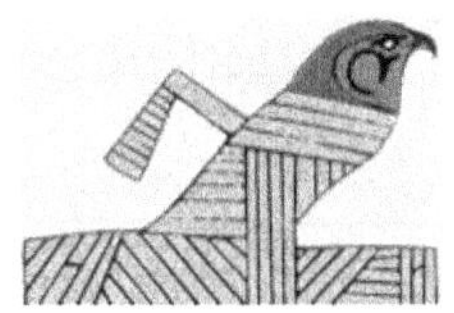

CHAPTER 15

I had the relics back, but all I could think about as I rode was Mehyt.

What was going to meet my eyes?

My mind conjured up horrors.

I saw Mehyt struggling in a tangle of wrappings that she was too weak to break free from, choked by cloth, suffocated before she could emerge, the dexterous skills of the mummy wrappers craft too much to overcome in spite of the linen's ancient state.

"Give me air to breathe," souls in the underworld pleaded.

She would have none.

What could be more airless than that shrouded mummy I had left in the sanctuary.

Unless... she had managed to break free...

In a symbol of nature echoing the drama of Osiris and his death and resurrection, Egyptians would shut little

Osiris images inside the tomb, seed trays fashioned in the outline of the god of the dead. Grain seeds left in moistened soil would germinate in darkness long after the tomb had been sealed... yet would perish in time without the sun to nourish them into further growth.

I pictured her lying weak and pale like a doomed seedling sprouted in a tomb only to yellow, wither and shrivel without sunlight.

I ran into the tomb sanctuary, bearing the monkey on my shoulder and the collection of relics in both arms, flying down the steps and lengths of passages like the rays of sunlight that had flashed from copper mirrors to reach me in my chamber.

I had never been this afraid.

Be alive, Mehyt, smiling, radiant, your eyes greeting me joyously.

Or be dead, safe in dreadful stillness, unharmed by my act of blasphemous folly...

Mehyt was there.

There was no sign of struggle.

She lay where I had left her.

Still a cut, dried flower.

I felt suffocated in my wrappings and my heart felt choked with sand.

I heard her whisperings.

"I love you, Hori, Great Hero of Egypt. One day, when your battles are won, we shall walk together again, hand in hand in the Fields of the Blessed - with that little monkey of yours on your shoulder. Console yourself that until that time our earthly bodies will lie side by side in your tomb sanctuary."

I had not been there when Mehyt died a thousand years earlier.

I mourned for her now.

Events interrupted my grief.

An emissary from the priesthood of Ra came with news.

He arrived at the sanctuary in a Hyksos chariot to tell me breathlessly of an urgent new danger.

King Apophis had rattled the knucklebones for one final throw of the dice against Egypt that could rip the land apart forever.

The priestly emissary, his eyes as round and watchful as an Egyptian owl's, said:

"Great Hori, you have already served Egypt beyond belief and the nation's gratitude, but another peril arises. Our spies inform us that Apophis plans to form an alliance with the Nubians in the South. He is sending a shipment of modern weaponry as a goodwill gift, as well as Egyptian gold looted from our tombs, hoping to win the Southerners to his cause. "Come, let us strike the serpent of the Nile at both ends - its head and its tail," he is telling them, "and we shall divide its riches between us."

"Foolish king," I said. "Doesn't he know that he is sending gold to the land of gold, and bows to the Land of the Bow, even though his bows are superior? Yet the risk is too great to ignore. How far has their boat come?"

"They will pass by on the river in hours. A ship disguised as a trader, but distinguishable by a red square sail."

"Then I will prepare. I shall begin this moment."

Something else had begun.

Decay and deterioration.

I noticed it as I gathered my weapons and took hold of a bow. My hands left powder on the weapon.

My skin was cracking, turning to dust.

I looked at my face in a copper mirror and a sigh escaped my lungs, a dry hiss like sand in a windstorm.

My reclaimed semblance of life and colour had faded.

You have risen for a time, Hori, but your life cannot be prolonged indefinitely and you must return to your rest.

So soon?

"I will need your help," I told the emissary.

We took Hyksos arrows and wrapped their ends in twists of cloth that I cut with a dagger from my wrappings. We found jars of volatile oils in my tomb sanctuary and we dipped the cloth in the pungent fluid.

Ironic.

I, the mummy, would be shooting arrows wrapped in the cloth of doom.

"Your hands shake, Great Hori," the watchful emissary said, noticing. "Is it weariness from your battles?"

"More than that. My time is ending and the process of entropy and decay has begun. It will fall to you to safeguard the relics and to lay me down to my rest after this fight is done. Then there is another task I would ask of you as an emissary. Go afterwards to Thebes to the two young royals, Kamose and Ahmose. Give them my message. They are to prepare a new fighting machine for Egypt with new weapons and tactics. Tell them to learn from the Hyksos. To borrow their skill in casting hardened bronze. To fashion compound bows made of wood, horn and sinew. To make better chariots, with lighter, skeletal bodies and wheels, so they are swifter and more agile in battle... With the rites of Egypt's resurrection now performed, they must use their new power to drive the Desert Dwellers back into the desert where they came from."

"Would that you could fight alongside them, Hori."

"This will be my last fight against the Hyksos. If my strength holds."

"I will pray to Ra for strength."

Strength.

Would I still have strength enough to bend a mighty Hyksos bow when the enemy vessel with its red sail crept into my sights?

Would the bow's added muscle of wood, horn and sinew fight against my arms?

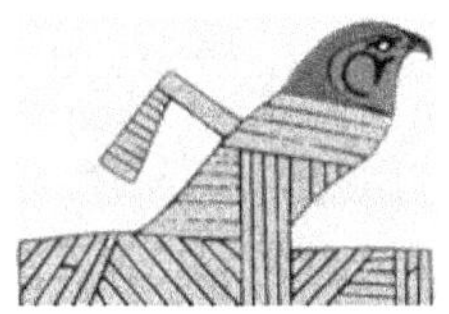

CHAPTER 16

A red sail on the river sent a greater spasm of fear into me than a fleet of Hyksos warships for now my arms and hands were trembling.

Slowly the vessel crept level with us.

We had used a flint to light an oil lamp and now the emissary, sheltering behind rock, held up the lamp for me to light the first arrow.

I gave the arrow a lick of the flame.

The cloth dipped in oils gulped in the flame and flared, but I could only guess how long it might burn in its flight across water to the boat.

Thoth peered over a rock at the Hyksos Boat like a spy.

I nocked the missile to the bowstring and held up the bow.

The vessel stood half the width of the river away. Only a Hyksos bow could reach it from our hiding place in the sand among rocks on the riverbank.

I took aim at the red sail, making minute allowances for breeze and the trajectory of flight and bent the bow, my arms trembling.

Further.

It must jump half a river.

I could hold no longer and released.

The arrow flew away like a panicked bird on fire, climbed, speeding on target… then plunged uselessly into the Nile.

The monkey gave a cry of dismay.

It would take more strength than I had.

I ground my teeth like millstones.

The wrappings on my body that gave me strength were binding my muscles, wrestling against my strength like constricting snakes.

"We are losing them, Mighty Hori!" the emissary said, despair in his voice.

Time had defeated me.

"Once a hero, you are no better than a Helpless One who must crawl on the sand," the monkey once told me as I lay on a hilltop overlooking a battle.

On the sand.

I rocked my body, tipped over, and fell with my back to the sand.

"Light another arrow and put the belly of the bow on my feet!" I hissed to the emissary.

Grasping my meaning, he sprang into action.

He placed the bow at my feet and put a flaming arrow in place. I raised my head and took hold of the bowstring, using the greater strength of my legs to bend the toughened wood, horn and sinew.

The fletching of the arrow crept back, back.

Wind and fall of arrow.

I made the swift allowances.

Now.

It flew.

We turned as motionless as stone as it flew.

It flew an age.

But it flew true.

A wisp of smoke snaked up from the red sail.

Monkey cheered.

Flames leapt and ran amok.

The Hyksos plans to forge an alliance with the Nubians in the South were going to sink to the bottom of the Nile.

I closed my eyes and rested on the hot dry sand.

Thoth came to me.

I felt the tiny weight of the creature squatting on my chest as rays of the sun struck the bindings around my stretched out body.

Incense from the land of Punt, the scent of the gods, wreathed the sanctuary with its fragrant smoke as the priest helped me back into my golden coffin near the resting form of Mehyt and he lifted Thoth from the floor so that he could curl up at my feet.
The monkey's limbs had grown stiff, his chattering ceased.
I lay with the monkey at my feet and a sword at my side.
"Rest the great rest you have earned, Mighty Hori," the priest said. "Egypt thanks you."
I heard a screech and a rumble and now the tomb sanctuary vanished as the golden lid slid over and brought thick darkness.
When would Egypt call on me to defend her again?

Book 2

I, the Archaeologist

The scribal writing kit, with mixing palette, pigment in a bag and reed pens in a pen case

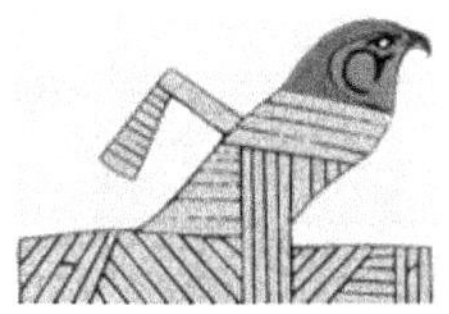

CHAPTER 17

Today, museum workers were removing the tomb contents for transport to the new Grand Egyptian Museum at the foot of the pyramids outside Cairo.

I stood at the tomb entrance, observing.

I was wilting, not only because of the furnace of the Egyptian sun in the afternoon.

Electric cables linked to thudding generators somewhere in the background ran cords like frightened snakes into the tomb while a parade of workers came out into the blazing hot sun, bearing tomb goods like merchants in a bazaar showing off their merchandise. They carried them over to a holding tent where they were to be prepared for loading on trucks in the morning. Animated Egyptian officials and bored looking antiquitics guards with machine guns looked on as well as a few members of the team. Others were down below supervising the wrapping and removal of tomb goods.

I was in mourning.

Did Hori have a presentiment that his tomb sanctuary might one day be invaded? Three thousand years after the rule of the Hyksos, our university archaeological team had uncovered him, along with his astonishing account written on scrolls.

"What is this place? A sanctuary? A tomb? Both?" our archaeology team leader Adam had said when we first opened the underground structure and made a sweeping examination by flashlight beam.

"A treasure house," I said.

"I don't see much evidence of that, Naomi," he said.

"Then look over there. Scrolls."

"Spoken like a papyrologist."

For archaeologists there were treasures far greater to be found than the buried hoard of gold and jewels in the tomb of Tutankhamun.

Texts.

Documents.

Studying them gave us the answers that we spent our careers searching for, shining a light of clarity on the past, while contemplating treasures merely dazzled the eyes like staring at the sun.

This was especially true for me, an Egyptologist specialising in ancient papyrus and written texts.

This underground tomb sanctuary reached by long passages and twisted stairways was a revelation. An armoury stocked with weapons and at its heart a golden coffin, while a withered female mummy lay stretched out nearby.

"The tomb owner must have been phenomenally important," said a bio-archaeologist who was poring over the coffin case with the hawk's head and wondering about the mummy inside. "It's rare that a coffin from a period of such vast antiquity as this would be anything but a severe oblong box, either in timber or stone. Yet it has a humanoid shape. He was clearly somebody, yet not a king. Who? There are no names carved on the case or anywhere I can see, or on the walls around him to give us a clue."

Compelling as these finds were, finding ancient scrolls, the rarest finds of all in a tomb, put the discovery in a category of its own.

Even at a glance I could tell from their astonishing condition that they were scrolls from a more recent age than the tomb, New Kingdom or even Ptolemaic.

"Scrolls from the primordial age of this sanctuary would be turning to dust by now," I said. "The tomb is too old for the scrolls, which makes them a riddle wrapped in a mystery, inside an enigma. Hieroglyphs would barely have been invented, although we keep pushing back the date of the advent of the earliest writing in ancient Egypt with new discoveries, but the first complete sentence written in hieroglyphs only dates to the second dynasty. These scrolls shouldn't be here unless they were added later. Do they even belong with the owner of this tomb?"

"Well he had a writing kit," the Egyptian antiquities inspector Hamad noted with his affable humour. "Look, here is a scribal kit, with mixing palette, pigment in a bag and reed pens in a pen case. And also spare sheets of papyrus."

"That writing kit is an anomaly too," I said. "New Kingdom by the look of it. So what on earth have we got here?"

Our bafflement deepened on the day that we slid back the hawk-headed lid of the coffin and shone our light beams inside.

The bio-archaeologist, Digby, gave a gasp.

It was a still-life of the macabre.

A powerful, impressively preserved mummy of a male lay stretched out inside, his features as rugged as a cliff face, a *kophesh* sickle sword at his side, its blade tarnished with a green patina of age, and, most unexpected of all, a bundle lying at his feet that we thought at first might be a swaddled baby, perhaps a still-born, until we saw a curling tail.

A mummified monkey.

"What in creation are we are looking at here?" the team leader said under his breath.

"Quite a few academic papers, I'd say," the biology expert said.

"A warrior and an ape."

"Technically an African long-tailed monkey," Digby, the bio-archaeologist said, "but yes, a warrior, judging by the wicked looking sword."

"Then that's an anomaly too," the expedition leader Adam said. "The bronze *khopesh* didn't make its appearance in Egypt until after the Hyksos invasion. So how are we going to unravel all this?"

"By unrolling the scrolls," I said. "They're in great shape. I'd like to tackle a translation. Until we do that we'll have no idea of what we're dealing with here."

Then my painstaking translations had begun and I settled down to unroll the riddle, wrapped in a mystery, inside an enigma.

The account of Hori was the most astonishing document that had ever come under my hand for translation.

The writing did not originate in the time of the Hyksos invasion, a period that followed the Middle Kingdom, I saw at once from the freshness of the pigment.

The scrolls had been written later.

How?

And by whom?

A revenant Hori?

Was I to believe his story literally?

Would anybody, let alone an academic like me or the members of my team believe it?

I felt a hand squeeze my shoulder as I stood in the sun watching the tomb slowly empty and recalling events that had led to today.

"Cheer up." It was Digby, the young English bio-archaeologist. "You have an air of lamentation. Why don't you just raise your arms and wail like Isis and Nephthys at the tomb of Osiris?"

"I've thought about it."

"I'm thinking your sadness is about more than the realization that the work here is coming to an end."

More Egyptian workers in *galabea* gowns came up the stone steps carrying Hori's cache of weapons in trays and I saw sunlight find a gleam on a tarnished and corroded blade of an Egyptian straight sword.

It reminded me of how the priests had used shining mirrors of copper to bounce sunlight into the tomb to bathe Hori and his pet monkey in warmth.

Reviving sunlight.

And soon they would be bringing Hori up too, hidden from the sunlight in his hawk-headed mummy case.

I sighed.

"I'm wondering, a little hypocritically perhaps for a professional Egyptologist, what Hori would have made of this latest invasion - the invasion of his resting place and the stripping of his tomb? This time not an invasion by an enemy armed with new weapons, but academics armed with degrees."

"You're not a hypocrite," he said. "A bit subversive maybe. You have some rebellious thoughts about our profession that are pretty damning for me. Digging up mummies and studying them is what I do."

I liked Digby and he had an amused toleration of my qualms. Though I was an Egyptologist like him and a papyrologist, I was clearly out of step with my profession. I was quite happy to unearth meaning in ancient texts, in scrolls, on walls and on monuments, but I had problems about digging up tombs and taking away their occupants to put on display.

"Tell me, Digby. Which is the more horrific story? That of a mummy rising to shed the blood of enemies and defend Egypt against oppressors?

Or the state-sanctioned excavation of his tomb, in the form of Egypt's Antiquities Department, aided by foreign mercenary archaeologists, stripping his tomb of its contents? All so that he can be put on show before the curious eyes of tourists in the new Grand Egyptian Museum?"

"It depends on whether you're facing that mummified monster armed with his sword dripping blood. Or gazing at him inside a glass case in the air-conditioned comfort of the museum. I know which I'd find more horrific."

"You know what I mean."

"Well, the first alternative is just a fantasy. I've studied mummies for years and even if you could rouse one, no mummy could ever run around swinging a sword or an axe. Their bodies and limbs are too stiff. In fact, a mummy's dried up joints, bones, cartilage and sinew would snap and splinter like old wood. Even though Old Hori happens to be in remarkable condition. Unlike his female companion who is sadly showing her age."

What were we to make of Hori's written account? I wondered.

Legend?

Myth?

Pure story?

The first work of sustained fiction in history?

Over the months of our stay in the desert, I spent laborious and ecstatic hours deciphering the scrolls, often at night alone in my tent by the light of a whispering gas lamp, but I still burnt with curiosity...
I wanted to know more.

If I was to take the story at its word, Hori must have risen again in order to have written down his account.

Had Egypt called on Hori again?

When?

Egypt had been conquered by a series of foreign empires long after the expulsion of the Hyksos, I recalled.

Did Egypt wake him from his long sleep to fight against the Assyrians?

Then against Egypt's neighbors the Nubians, when they rose to conquer and save a weakened Egypt from itself and ruled their former masters for seventy-five years, becoming in the process as Egyptian as the Egyptians? Did Egypt call on its defender to take up the sword and the bow against the Persian conqueror Cambyses, a thousand years after the Hyksos invasion? And again in the age of the Ptolemies that began with the conquest of Egypt by Alexander the Great and ended under

Cleopatra when ancient Egypt finally lost its freedom to the might of Rome?

Then where were these accounts?

Perhaps Hori set out to write the long record of his struggles for Egypt, beginning with his first battle against the Hyksos, only to weary of the telling.

We would never know.

Hori was coming out of the tomb.

I saw the martial beak of the hawk appear, then the hawk's head and the bulk of the coffin emerge, the warrior Hori carefully brought out of his grave into the heat of the Egyptian day, borne by four men like pall-bearers at a funeral ceremony that was happening in reverse.

'Greetings, Hori,' I thought. 'I say your name and you will live and not die the second death. I speak your name out loud...'

"Hori."

I wished him loaves of bread and jars of beer and wine...

Hori was here.

He was 'Coming Forth by Day', I thought. The Book of Coming Forth By Day, I reminded myself, was the technical name for what was popularly known as the Book of the Dead.

Then, as I sent my wishes to the body inside the ancient coffin, an event exploded my sentimental reverie and ripped open the afternoon.

The ear-puncturing blast of a bomb, it sounded like, and it was followed by a clatter of machine gun fire.

We thought it was a terrorist attack and a guard somewhere with a nervous finger on a machine gun trigger thought so too.

The cause was less dramatic, but equally dangerous. A generator had exploded. Somebody had overfilled a fuel tank and with the great heat of the day the pressure in the tank expanded to critical levels and the generator exploded.

Yet it might as well have been a full-scale attack by dissidents for the panic it caused.

Egyptians, officials and workmen, were yelling and running everywhere.

Digby grabbed my arm.

"Better lie low, Naomi."

He led me behind a truck where he shoved me down beside him to take cover.

"Suppose it had to happen some day," he said through gritted teeth.

An Egyptian official ran to us. "Stay where you are, don't move. We are on the radio for police and army and they will be here soon."

We waited.

The first gunshots now triggered other nervous fingers and there were more stutters of machine gun fire.

"I'll bet Old Hori wasn't expecting a ten gun salute."

"Why would they attack us?" I said.

"Well it's not because they have more respect for antiquities than we do, We've seen how terrorists treat ancient heritage."

I don't know how long we stayed pinned behind the truck before police and military help arrived in roaring trucks and the cause of the panic was finally identified. The Egyptian Antiquities Inspector explained rather sheepishly that a generator had unfortunately exploded although he did not bother to explain the response of machine gun fire.

"If that didn't wake up your friend, Naomi, nothing will," Digby said.

Hori!

They had been carrying his coffin out of the tomb sanctuary when the explosion had ripped through the valley.

I said his name out aloud once again.

"Hori!"

"You like saying his name," Digby said.

Yes, I did, but this time it was in fear, not reverence.

"I've just had an alarming thought. In all the panic and commotion - do you think he made it safely to the holding tent?"

That panicked the bio-archaeologist as much as the explosion.

He ran to the tomb entrance and I followed him.

The unthinkable had happened.

CHAPTER 18

In the hot flame of panic, the Egyptian bearers had dropped Hori's coffin.

It had landed so precipitously that it had fallen on its side, breaking open and disgorging its contents onto the sand.

The mummy of Hori, his *khopesh* sword, and the little bundle of the monkey lay there under the full blaze of the Egyptian sun.

How long had it been?

Digby shouted for help and two of the team members lifted Hori, his sword and the monkey back into the case. Shamefaced workers helped replace the lid and they carried Hori into the holding tent.

"Hopefully no harm done by the look of him," Digby said. "A fall doesn't help, but the drying heat of the sun is not the real enemy of mummies. It's humidity and moisture that wreaks havoc."

"And fire. I'm glad he was nowhere near the generator that blew."

"I'll keep a check on his state. See if there's any deterioration in his condition."

Living so closely with Hori and his story in the process of translation - the papyrus fibre crackling as if alive under my hand - I felt as if I had entered into a special relationship with him. Some of that magical wrapping had bound me to him, a state that could only come from living so long and so intimately with his words and thoughts.

I was shaking after the accident.

How close to catastrophe his precious remains had come!

And to think that his body had been left lying in the blaze of the sun.

What an irony.

The revivifying sun, agent of his rising in the story.

I imagined the sun's penetrating warmth entering the dryness of his bones, muscles, cartilage and sinew.

I drew a breath of air into my dried up lungs, he had written, *like a hiss of sand in a windstorm, forced my eyelids open, cracking a seal of dust and time. Light roared in my skull. My eyes cowered at the shining fire as I peered out from between gaps in frayed linen bandaging.*

At the corners of my eyes, loose threads of cloth frayed with age turned into blazing filaments of light.

Sunlight!

But the sun did not bring the long, long dead to life and mummies didn't rise.

Except in the realms of story.

Yet many of the factual details of Hori's account had checked out. The presence of the monkey and the *khopesh* sword in the coffin case, the mummy of the young woman Mehyt lying nearby him, the tomb sanctuary and cache of weapons just as he had described them.

It was a tomb dinner, an Egyptian style evening organised by our local colleagues to mark the end of the season.

We sat on campstools and on the warm sand beside rugs spread with Egyptian dishes, spicy *kebab, falafels* and *fava* beans, baked white fish and *baladi* flat bread along with a herb-filled creamy dip called *besara*.

"How is Hori?" I asked Digby as he bent to dip a jagged flap of bread in the dip.

"Still in one piece," he said. "I'll do a final check on him before bedtime. After tomorrow he's going to be the Grand Museum's concern."

"And the monkey Thoth is okay?"

He nodded.

"Fine. Odd though, Hori taking a pet with him on his eternal journey."

"Pets make wonderful travelling companions," I said, "and it seems from Hori's account that Thoth was the ultimate companion animal. I've decided to think of this as a dinner in honour of the two of them, like the customary feasts that mourning ancient Egyptians held in front of tomb chapels. Just a pity they've been evicted."

"What a combination you are, Naomi, a sentimentalist and a rebel."

That night, alone in my tent, I missed the scrolls that I had been allowed to handle with infinite care in my translation, but they had now gone to the white coat specialists for scientific preservation.

Yet the words of Hori lived with me.

In the grainy scrolls of the papyrus I had seen the rusty linen fibres of his wrappings and I dreamt sometimes that I was reading Hori like an unfolding book and that the writing was on his body and wrapped around him and I was peeling away layers to reach the truth.

Monster or Defender?

I had seen the humanity in him. Yet he was a violent killer by his own admission.

I have killed men.

I have avenged myself and burnt with rage.

I have stolen what belongs to gods and goddesses.

I have behaved with violence.

Now the Defender of Egypt would soon become just an exhibit, a number and a label on a museum case.

I felt a wild impulse to rescue him from that. Load him on a truck and drive him so far into the desert that nobody would ever find him and there in some place of utter solitude, give him a final secret burial.

Egyptologists didn't do things like that.

But they could dream about it.

I was still dreaming about it, resting fully clothed on my camp stretcher, when I heard an alarmed yelling disturb the quietness of the camp.

I ran.

"The holding tent. A terrible situation," the Egyptian Inspector said.

I went to the tent, joining others bringing lights.

It was a scene of carnage.

Our temporary storeroom, the holding tent, had been turned into an ancient Egyptian embalmers' tent with bodies of armed guards strewn like corpses awaiting the embalmers' attention, heads and throats slashed.

I found Digby, clutching a rusted Egyptian sword in his hand as he lay stretched out, skull split open.

Who...?"

My first thought was that armed thieves had invaded the tent. What had they taken?

My eyes and a pencil flashlight I took from a pocket converged on the coffin of Hori.

The lid - shoved aside.

I ran to look inside.

Empty.

The Inspector was at my shoulder.

"They have taken him."

They had done nothing.

Maybe, somehow, I had brought this evil on them through some kind of enacted magic in my translation of his story, I thought, as I went alone into the desert, my thin beam tracking a set of footprints.

It was as if I had brought his story to life and therefore a spectre to life.

Words were things that had power the ancient Egyptians believed.

The spell did not exist until it was spoken.

The dead did not live unless their names were living on the tongues of men.

Illogical?

Not to the Egyptians.

There was an invisible skein that linked the written and spoken word with reality and if you found that link and drew on it, you could produce events in the real world and I had drawn on that skein, like Nepthys creating substance from wisps of thread and magic on her divine loom.

I was following that invisible skein now.

It bound me to Hori.

I could feel him in the night like a tug.

Stalk as far as you like with that monkey on your shoulder. I will find you.

And then...?

I did not know yet.

But I wanted to wind in the thread of this mystery so that I would know the truth about ancient magic and evil.

Would he carry a blooded sword?

The Hyksos *khopesh* that had been in the coffin beside him?

Oh, Hori.

Oh, Digby.

My bond was with both of them.

This was the worst kind of tragedy and horror.

Too horrible to believe... and therefore impossible?

Perhaps I was following the trail left by some deranged dissident with a grudge against Egyptology.

I rejected that.

The dangers of terrorists had vaporized earlier that afternoon, like the fumes in the fuel tank of the generator that had exploded our lives apart.

If I find him, he could kill me too, I thought.

But it wasn't exactly fear that I was experiencing.

I felt wrapped in an enthralled, and enthralling, wonder.

My torch picked out the depressions of footprints in the sand.

A man's size, yet shallower than expected for a man of his size.

The monkey on his shoulder would add little weight.

What would I say? What could I say?

Just because I had translated his words did not translate me into his world or he into mine.

Papyrologists could master all the glyphs and grammar of the past without ever knowing how the ancients sounded or spoke. Some believed that the ancient Egyptian spoken language would have been softer and more mellifluous than the guttural Arabic of today's Egyptian.

I did not care. It was not words I wanted. I'd had enough of those. I'd written enough of those. Thought enough of those.

I want to *see* whatever was there in the eyes of the living-dead warrior.

Could I withstand the existential terrors of such a meeting?

Would it be like facing a ghost? I wondered if he would sense that I meant him no harm in spite of what he had done. Perhaps the armed antiquities guards in the holding tent had provoked him and, true to his nature, he attacked.

And Digby?

I could only guess that the archaeo-biologist had arrived to make a final check on his condition for the night, witnessed the violent attack under way and reached for one of the ancient swords taken from the tomb...

The warrior, armed with the *khopesh* sword, had struck again.

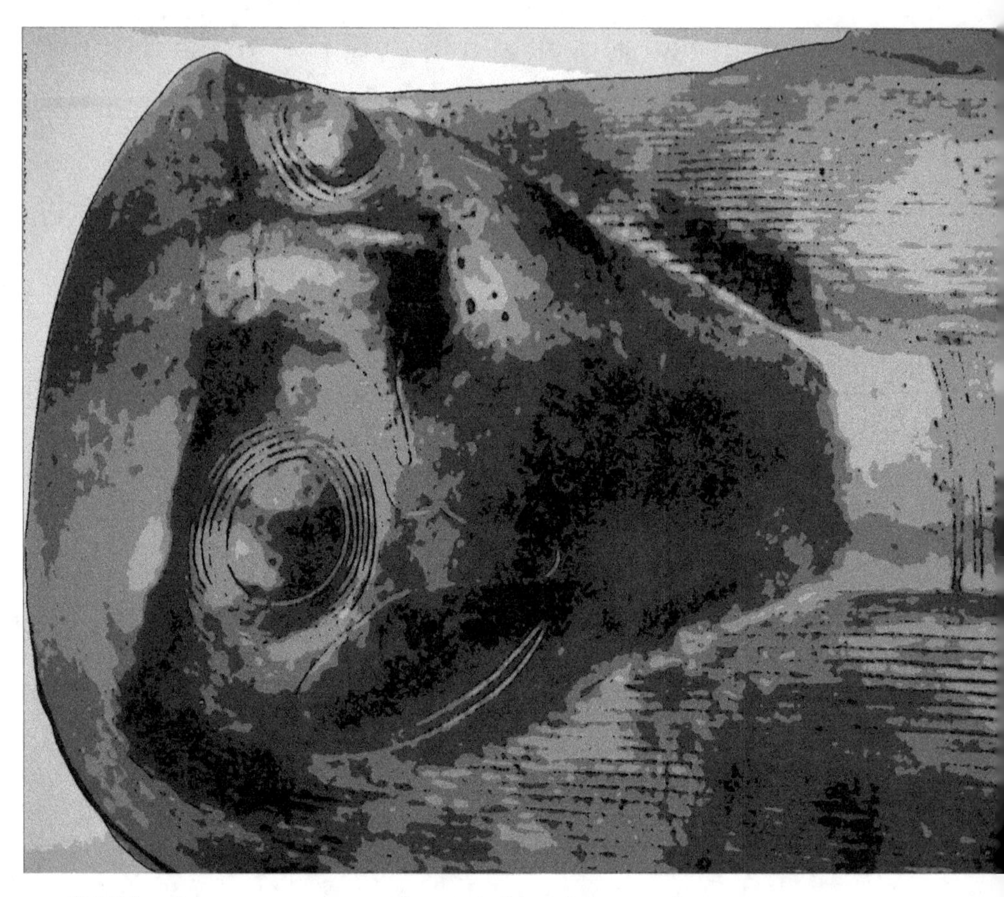

Did he have a presentiment that his tomb sanctuary might be invaded?

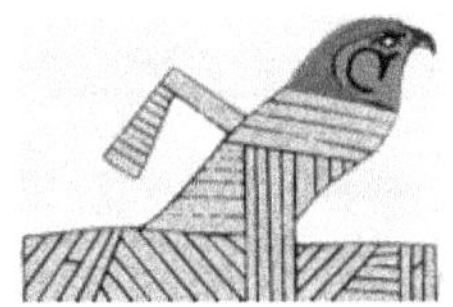

CHAPTER 19

A moon had risen.

I came upon the distant form of a shadowy hulk walking in a stretch where the sand shimmered like moonbeams on the sea.

He cast a look back over his shoulder.

Was it threatening?

Reproving?

Puzzled at my persistence?

He did not stop, but now something else marked the trail of footsteps.

Scraps... of bandage.

The hero whose life I had tracked on the written page was leaving a kind of paper trail behind him, shreds, curls, lengths of linen wrapping.

I recalled the warning of the High Priest in his story.

"Your eyes shall see, Hori," the Chief Prophet Of Ra said. "But first gather your strength. Allow Ra's beneficent

rays of fire to revivify your limbs. Then you may rise to this new age of war, though taking care never to shed your armour of divine bands. The Tresses of Nephthys and the Knotted Cords of Isis around your body are the secrets of your strength and miraculous preservation."

He was shedding his wrappings, like a snake sloughing its dead skin.

Why?

This was not some shedding in preparation for a new phase of life, I guessed.

Then what?

A new, permanent death?

The Defender was destroying himself, slashing and tugging at his wrappings, discarding the wrappings of Nephthys and the Knotted Cords of Isis.

And yes, the monkey on his shoulder was doing the same, unwinding its bands.

The two of them were shedding their past in the moonlit trail.

That was when I decided.

I couldn't go on.

I stopped.

It would be wrong to follow them now.

Allow them this, in spite of all.

I watched the warrior and the monkey fade from my view in the sand.

About Roy Lester Pond

Roy Lester Pond is a prolific author of ancient Egypt-inspired fiction. His depth of knowledge comes from a lifetime spent studying ancient Egypt and Egyptian archaeology. He has been to Egypt on numerous research trips. Roy is fascinated by the mystery of ancient Egypt and its potency and relevance for today's world. 'The Smiting Texts' was his first archaeological thriller, followed by a series featuring renegade Egyptologist Anson Hunter, as well as other stand-alone adventures. Roy spent much of his life in Africa and now lives in Australia. Roy Tweets regularly about Egypt and adventure fiction writing under the Twittername "Egyptsnippets" and writes a blog 'Ancient Egypt

Fiction&Facts'.

Mystery of Egypt Collection by Roy Lester Pond

The Egyptian adventure series featuring Anson Hunter, alternative Egyptologist, battling dangers from the ancient past:-

ROY LESTER POND
THE SMITING TEXTS
HATHOR'S HOLOCAUST
ROY LESTER POND
THE IBIS APOCALYPSE
ROY LESTER POND
A BOATLOAD OF EGYPTOLOGISTS, A NIGHT OF DIVINE JUDGEMENT
THE NIGHT OF ANUBIS CRUISE
ROY LESTER POND
ROY LESTER POND
THE FORBIDDEN GLYPHS
EGYPT EYES
ANSON HUNTER ARCHAEOLOGY THRILLER
Roy Lester Pond
ROY LESTER POND
THE GOD DIG
ARTEFACT
ROY LESTER POND
AN ANSON HUNTER THRILLER
ALEXANDER'S LOST EGYPTIAN ORACLE
ROY LESTER POND

New

THE ANSON HUNTER series or archaeological mystery
adventures

Hidden dangers from Egypt's past, modern-day
conspiracies that take their impetus from Egypt's
ancient mysteries.

The Smiting Texts, Hathor's Holocaust, The Ibis Apocalypse, Hidden Egypt - The Night of Anubis, Egypt Eyes, The Forbidden

The first three Anson Hunter novels in the 9-novel series – in one Kindle edition. Fiction's favourite independent, renegade Egyptologist. The Smiting Texts, Hathor's Holocaust, The Ibis Apocalypse
*****5-star fiction Amazon/Goodreads

THE EGYPTIAN MYTHOLOGY MURDERS

A mummy named Isis is taken to a hospital for a non-invasive imaging scan... so begins a mystery and a string of deaths.

An ancient cycle unfolds in modern day London - and a search for eternal love.

Can Jennefer, a young trainee museum curator and Jon, a police antiquities unit detective, stop the killings in time before a terrible culmination of events?

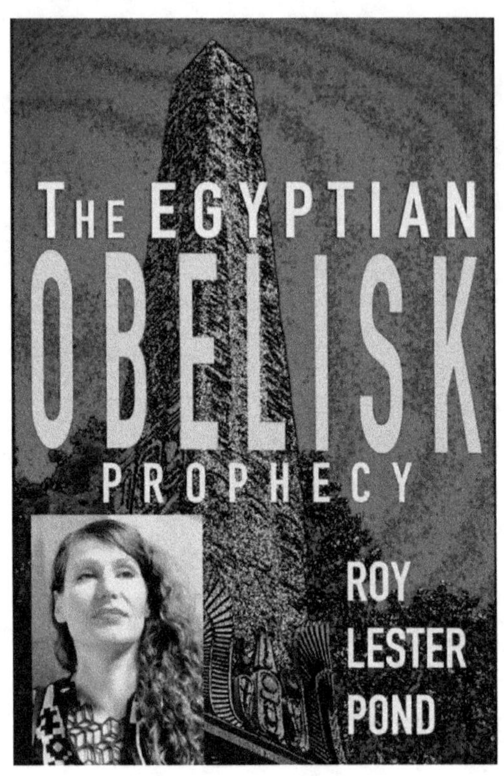

The EGYPTIAN OBELISK Prophecy

What was the Obelisk Prophecy?

The exciting fiction sequel to 'The Egyptian Mythology Murders'.

Detectives and Egyptologists are in sister professions. Now the unusual team of Jennefer, an Egyptologist museum curator, and Jon, an arts and antiquities policeman, is back together in 'The Obelisk Prophecy". Egyptian obelisks are potent symbols that pierce the skies around the world. London, New York, The Vatican...

But now one obelisk represents the clue to a world-threatening mystery.

Working against secret enemies the team must race to find and penetrate the riddle of the one obelisk on earth that holds the key to salvation.

THE EGYPTIAN CROCODILE QUEEN

When a new blockbuster ancient Egyptian exhibition arrives, mysterious events and a string of killings soon follow.

The investigative team of Jennefer, a curator, and Jon a police antiquities detective, must track down the

shocking truth in a hidden underworld beneath the city
- and discover a shocking secret from ancient Egypt,
linked to a modern day conspiracy that takes its
impetus from the ancient past.

In the unnerving footsteps of THE EGYPTIAN
MYTHOLOGY MURDERS and THE OBELISK
PROPHECY.

THE EGYPTIAN MUMMY WRAP MURDERS

4th book in the enthralling 'Egyptian Mythology
Murders' mystery series.
The spell of a vintage reel of film shot at a dig site in
Egypt in the early 1900s.
A crumbling mummy in the private museum collection
of a Grand English Castle today.

A mummy called Nephthys, the same name as the Egyptian goddess who wove the cloth mummy wrappings of Osiris, called the 'Tresses of Nephthys'.

A series of graphic murders...

Is the terrifying onslaught building to an event that will affect the world?

And what is the secret of the eerie, nonverbal young daughter of the Earl?

Investigative team of Jennefer, a British Museum Egyptologist Curator, and her partner Jon, an Antiques Unit Detective, have just hours to stop a countdown to catastrophe.

TRILOGY. THE EGYPTIAN MYTHOLOGY MURDERS: 3 TITLES IN ONE EDITION

Ancient Egypt resurrected...

3 Egyptian mythology driven mystery thrillers set in the modern day, but with a twist of the ancient unknown.

A unique investigative team of Jennefer, a museum curator, and Jon a London antiquities detective - two very different people who work in 'kindred professions'...

The X-Files meets 'The Mummy'...

- THE EGYPTIAN MYTHOLOGY MURDERS

A mummy named Isis is taken to a hospital for a non-invasive imaging scan... so begins a mystery and a string of deaths.

An ancient cycle unfolds in modern day London - and a search for eternal love.

Can Jennefer, a young trainee museum curator and Jon, a police antiquities unit detective, stop the killings in time before a terrible culmination of events?

- OBELISK One Egyptian obelisk is the key to saving civilization

- THE CROCODILE QUEEN MYSYERY An Egypt exhibition, a series of mythological murders

ARCHAEOLOGIST DETECTIVE SERIES

THE EGYPTOLOGIST DETECTIVE SERIES.

Meet Daniel Cane, archaeologist and sometimes cruise Egyptologist, who finds himself digging for murder clues in Egypt instead of for buried artefacts.

MURDER ON THE NILE MYSTERY CRUISE

MURDER IN NUBIA

ARCHAEOLOGY OF MURDER

THE SHABTI DOLL MURDERS

THE SARCOPHAGUS

Adventure, mystery, fantasy. An archaeologist with a
bow shoots an arrow into adventure...
In the modern age, Ryder an archaeologist in Egypt
discovers a mysterious empty sarcophagus in a tomb.
Then his Egyptologist partner Janet goes missing.
He vows to go after her, even if it means journeying
across the boundaries of reason and existence. Ahead of
Ryder and his Ridgeback dog lies a pre-dynastic realm
of myth: the mysterious Mistress of the Bow and Ruler
of Arrows, the evil Lord Set, legions of animal-headed
creatures, the venerable bird-man, the child Horus. And
key to it all is the quest for the magical amulets of

power. A life-and-death struggle is on at the edge of
time. And the universe watches - and waits.

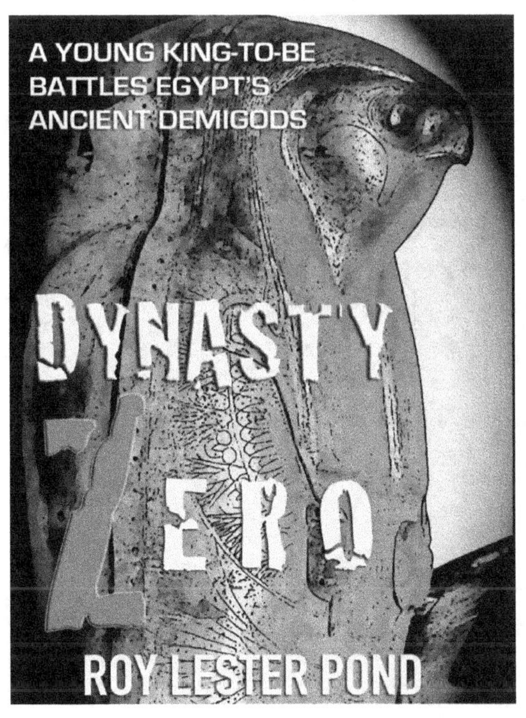

DYNASTY Zero

A primordial clash of humans, gods and demon demigods.

A young demigod boy Nemes, a future unifier of pharaonic Egypt, also known to history as Narmer, lived on the fault line between deity and humanity. It was a time of the gods and demigods, when the throne of the god Horus shook and the weak hands of men stretched out to catch the crown and seize the scepter of Egypt. The demon demigods did not stand by, but seized the moment to strike.

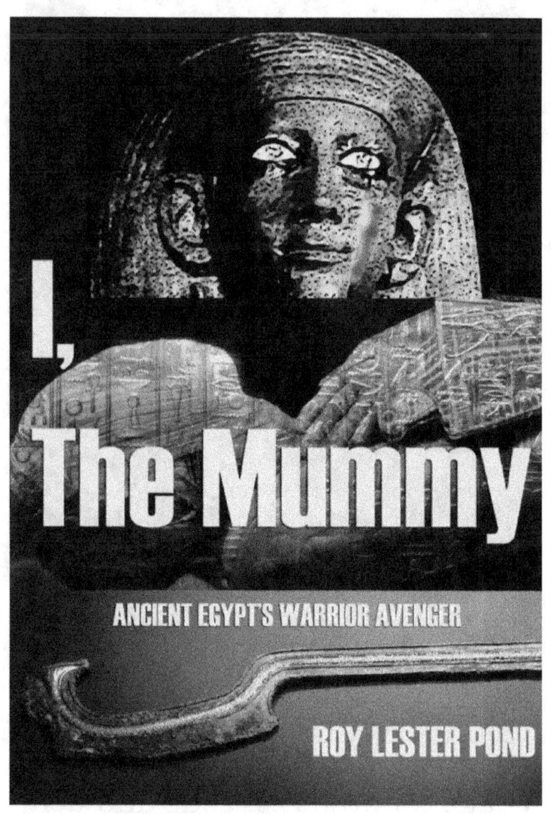

I, THE MUMMY

Preserved in the 'Tresses of Nephthys' - the sacred wrappings of linen woven by the goddess Nephthys and tied with the'magic of knotted cords' of Isis, an immortal soldier hero rises to fight Egypt's greatest enemy - the ruthless Hyksos invaders and occupiers...

Action adventure thriller.

Awakened after a thousand years in a tomb sanctuary filled with weapons...

The Ancient Defender arises to fight against a ruthless oppressor.

The Hyksos have seized Egypt at a time of weakness following the Middle Kingdom, overpowering all with their superior technology of chariots, hardened bronze weapons and compound bows.

And they are now plundering Egypt for its forbidden secrets of power.

Can ancient history's most unlikely hero stop them and resurrect a divided land before the Hyksos can gain Egypt's most powerful and dangerous secret of all?

THE RA VIRUS

Is a vanished archaeology team member trapped in Egypt's ancient past during an age of terror – and sending warning messages to today?

'WARNING! ANCIENT GLOBAL THREAT...' the graffiti message appears in a newly found Egyptian tomb, along with a modern biohazard symbol.

What mysterious plague has hit the population of Egypt in the reign of Pharaoh Amenhotep III and his young co-regent, the sun-struck Akhenaten? Why is it seen as a judgement by the angry sun god Ra? An eleventh plague of Egypt?

Lucas, a physician and World Health Organisation expert on pandemics, must find its source and the antidote in time to save the ancient past and the future. Especially when his lover, Egyptologist Giulietta in the modern age, is exposed to the deadly contagion. Can he warn her in time and save her - and can they ever hope to be reunited?

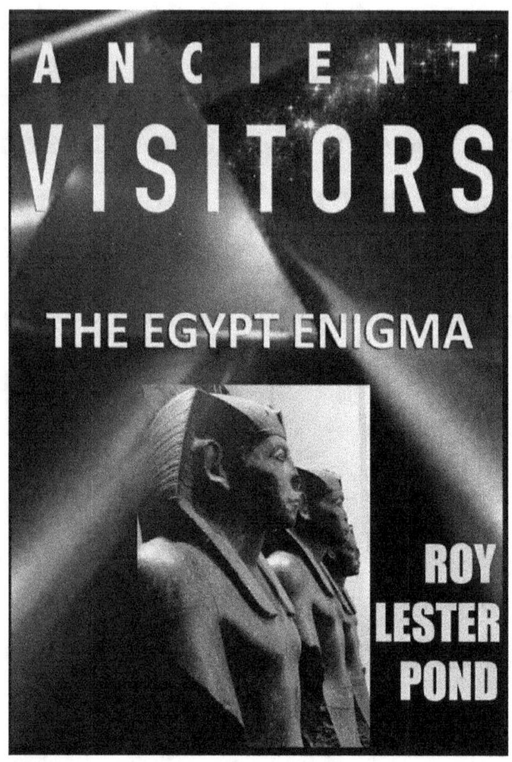

'Ancient VISITORS The Egypt Enigma'

In the field of ancient civilizations, 'visitors' meant one thing to Egyptologist Rebecca Landers.

The controversial theory about the enigma of Egypt and its advanced technological achievements.

Then came the surprising evidence... and a threat to the world.

Suddenly she and her team were called on to span two worlds on a dangerous archaeological quest like no other.

Only they had the power to save history and the future.

EGYPT EXTRACTION

TIME JUMP ERA: 3 A.D.

MISSION: Save the Jesus child, a refugee in Egypt, journeying with escaped family.

THREAT: modern day Islamic Time-Terrorists and ancient assassins of Judean King Herod...

Time-travel terrorists... drones... attackers with assault weapons racing through the Nile's papyrus reeds... their target a boy king.

At stake, the future of civilization.

Standing in their way, two young time jumpers, Salome and Callen of the Anti Time-Terrorist Strike Force. They must stop a catastrophe that could affect billions of lives and the belief systems of the world. Sci-fi, ancient history and time-travel novella with a startling twist and revelation.

Plus AVATAR EGYPT

An ancient Egyptian simulator game turns deadly real.

EGYPT TRAP

Keep an eye on a mysteriously obsessed young wife

visiting the archaeology sites of Egypt? How hard could

that be?

A damaged ex-detective is hired to shadow a girl with

painted eyes on a trip to Egypt...

Is she leading him step by step into a murder

conspiracy and the mystery of a lost ancient Egyptian queen?

Dan Loader reluctantly accepts the job. A damaged, former-detective from a police Art and Antiques unit, he is already traumatised by an ordeal at the hands of antiquity traffickers. Yet he desperately needs something to help him hold his life together and following the girl looks like a soft surveillance task, more so as he becomes increasingly drawn to her.

Rich, independent Kate Barnsdale is a beautiful, haunting young woman surrounded by an unmistakeable aura of ancient Egypt. Her obsession with a lost, mythic Queen from Egypt's 6th Dynasty seems to be taking over her life.

When she insists on travelling to Egypt alone to follow her mysterious urgings, her husband hires Dan to shadow her secretly and watch over her.

But is Dan being drawn step by step into a murder conspiracy that involves the secret of a mythic queen from Egypt's ancient past?

Crime and suspense with the mystery twist of ancient Egypt.

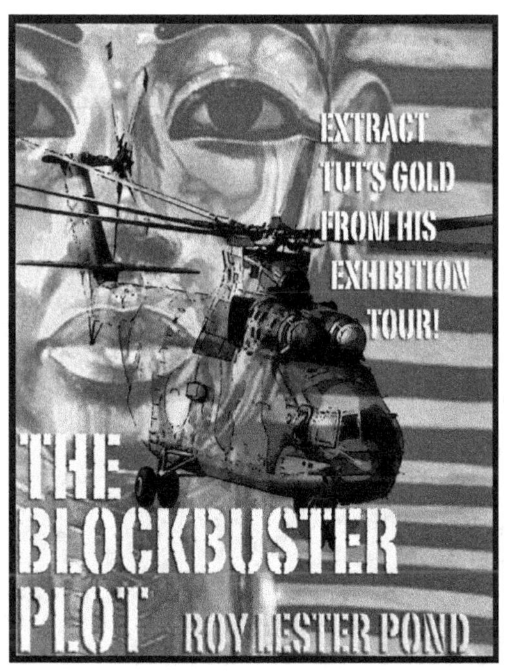

THE BLOCKBUSTER PLOT

The Boy King's Gold… a Blockbuster USA Tour… a dazzling display of criminal daring.

It was an outrageous plot:- Extract Tutankhamun's priceless gold on its blockbuster tour of the USA. *But who is the enigmatic mastermind behind the disappearing act and why have they done it?*

Will they demand a pharaoh's ransom for its return? And what will become of a pair of US hostages, a museum Egyptologist and a female National Geographic feature writer traveling with the treasures?

A golden target, the most famous treasures in the world… *gone…* the fabulous golden artefacts of

Tutankhamun, about to appear in the USA in the biggest blockbuster exhibition since the world wide pandemic, have been stolen.

ONE DAY I'LL TELL YOU SOMETHING

A child obsessed with the ancient past, a young mother who discovers adventure... "

I remember Egypt," Cooper said gravely. "Long, long ago."

Her little boy was gorgeous, she thought, but his imagined past life could be a bit hard to take. Especially at 8.30 in the morning, when she was busy having a this-life crisis, running late for work and her eight-year old was about to miss his school bus.Then young single-mother Catherine meets a past life researcher and also a mysterious Egyptologist Simon Priestly and she and Cooper are off to Egypt on an extraordinary quest to follow a young boy's dreams… or are they actual memories of the ancient past?

What will they find and what will Catherine find as she warms to the impressive British Egyptologist as they uncover a shattering secret from Egypt's past? Disturbing and intriguing adventure fiction with a twist of the unknown.

THE VIRTUAL EGYPT GAME - a group plays a deadly virtual reality running game inside a mysterious simulator of ancient Egypt's dangerous underworld. Then they start dying, for real.

THE GHOST OF THE BRITISH MUSEUM

There is a certain statue in the Sculpture Gallery of the
British Museum of the son of Rameses The Great,
Egypt's most illustrious pharaoh.
The statue has an eerie attraction even today.
In the 1900s a London group known as The Society of
Inner Light regularly conferred with the exhibit in the
Egyptian Sculpture Gallery, convinced that it was a
medium for metaphysical activity and emanated unseen

forces.

She was an American historical writer visiting the British Museum's Egyptian Sculpture Gallery to research a new book.

He was a legendary and enigmatic prince from ancient Egypt who desperately needed to undo a terrible mistake.

Was the strange young man's sudden materialization before Madeline just 'cosplay', or the result of an attraction between two souls across time?

Would they share a mysterious quest on a journey through Egypt, and much more?

THE PRINCESS WHO LOST HER SCROLL OF THE
DEAD

2 Egypt Fantasy Titles in One.

1. The Princess Who Lost Her Scroll of the Dead

Her priceless Book of the Dead is swapped for a blank
one by a greedy royal scribe... How can Ncfcra find her
way through the dangerous gateways and guardians of
the Egyptian underworld without her magical spells -
her passport to the world beyond?

And who is the boy tomb robber Ipy, sharing her

journey? Is he alive, or dead?

2.

MUSEUM GHOSTS

Karoy and his companions - a squad of Egyptian wooden soldiers created to protect a tomb owner - arise when the Lady Tiy is stolen from the museum. Can they rescue her from the outside world?